# HALF & HALF

A Collection of Short Stories & True Stories

Don Reid

HALF & HALF
A COLLECTION OF SHORT STORIES & TRUE
STORIES

*PUBLISHED BY*: REID PARTNERSHIP

P.O. BOX 2834
STAUNTON, VA 24402

Copyright © 2015
Don Reid
Reid Partnership
All rights reserved. Except for brief excerpts for review purposes,
this book, or parts thereof, may not be reproduced in any form
without permission.

ISBN 978-0-9914544-4-0

Printed in the United States

Cover design: aaron tinsley

# DEDICATION

To
My love and inspiration, Debbie, who says,
"If you smile, even when you don't feel like it,
your heart will catch up with your face."
And she lives by it.

Other Books by Don Reid

---

*Heroes & Outlaws of the Bible*

*Sunday Morning Memories*

*You Know It's Christmas When…*
(with Debo Reid & Langdon Reid)

*Random Memories*
(with Harold Reid)

*O Little Town*

*One Lane Bridge*

*The Mulligans of Mt. Jefferson*

DonReid.net

# FIRST HALF – FICTION

| | |
|---|---|
| FRIENDS | 5 |
| REVENGE | 9 |
| HOME | 12 |
| DEBT | 16 |
| MURDER | 22 |
| COURAGE | 27 |
| COWBOY | 29 |
| CHERRY | 33 |
| LUNCH | 38 |
| CARDS | 42 |
| FLAG | 47 |
| GREEN | 51 |
| RAN | 55 |
| RACE | 60 |
| SURPRISE | 64 |
| HENS | 68 |
| ROAD | 73 |
| BUNGLE | 77 |
| DIFFICULT | 81 |
| CHARITY | 85 |

# SECOND HALF – NONFICTION

| | |
|---|---|
| BICYCLE | 93 |
| SNOW | 95 |
| RAIN | 97 |
| TELEPHONE | 100 |
| BOOKS | 102 |
| GUITAR | 105 |
| UNCLE | 108 |
| FIRE | 111 |
| FORTUNE | 113 |
| GHOST | 116 |
| HOMESICK | 119 |
| SNAKE | 121 |
| SUMMER | 123 |
| SPAGHETTI | 125 |
| ACCIDENT | 127 |
| PANIC | 130 |
| TEACHER | 133 |
| RING | 136 |
| KEY | 138 |
| CHARITY | 141 |
| ABOUT THE AUTHOR | 144 |

# INTRODUCTION

This book you are about to read started as a game between two friends.

My brother, Harold, and I eat lunch with a friend of ours, Charles Culbertson, as often as his schedule will allow. Charles is an ex-newspaperman and writes a history column for our Staunton, VA newspaper, so as you might imagine, lots of our lunchtime conversation is about our love of writing, books and authors. In discussing the difference in fiction and non-fiction writing one day, he and I came up with a little game. We referred to it as our One Word Challenge. The rules were simple. He would think of a word and we both would have to write 800 to 1000 words about a true experience from our lives using that word as a theme. We would then email each other the story, critique and analyze it with one another and then I would send him the next word. The game continued and gave us lots of subjects to laugh about and jaw about over the next scheduled lunches.

After a while, we took the game to another level to explore our subjects further. We continued to give one another one-word titles but now we had to write a fictional short story instead of a real life story. Some stories we returned the next day but the harder ones often took as much as a week. But this little exercise (that every writing class should adopt and maybe you would like to try with a friend) led to two things. Charles hit on a character he used multiple times whom I found intriguing. I encouraged him to flesh out this guy and write a book around him. We stopped the game at that point so he could do just that and the sample chapters I have read tells me he has a fantastic book in the making. I hope it will be something that will hit the market and can be shared with every one of you soon.

# Don Reid

Now the other people I take lunch with on a regular basis are my two sons, Debo and Langdon. (Sounds like I eat a lot, doesn't it?) We make it a point to do this at least once a week without fail. So, in telling them about this little literary game I was involved in, they asked to read some of the stories. The next week they came back saying they thought it would be a perfect theme for a book. A book like no other any of us had ever seen. A book consisting of an equal mixture of short stories and true stories. Fact and fiction under the same cover. After some consideration, I agreed they might have a good idea. They put their talents to work producing the book from scratch. They put the format together and saw to all publishing and marketing and assured me I had nothing more to do. Liking the sound of that, I turned it all over to them and ordered another sandwich.

My only question to them was, "Under what section will this book be found in book stores? Fiction or Non-Fiction?" They suggested we might create a new genre altogether. Maybe call it True Fiction. So as you begin reading these pages, note that Part One is all short story fiction and Part Two is all true stories from my life. Some are very personal accounts because I had no intention of ever publishing them when I wrote them. They were strictly for the eye of my friend. I hope there is something here you'll enjoy and relate to. They were fun doing and as soon as Charles finishes his novel, who knows, we might do some more.

--Don Reid
On a bright October morning in 2015

# FIRST HALF

## fic·tion
ˈfik-shun
*noun*

    literature in the form of prose, especially short stories and novels, that describes imaginary events and people.

# FRIENDS

Sanchez and Eddie were best friends. Mainly, because no one else wanted to hang with either one of them. Freshly turned 18, they had quit school just a week apart with the promise of finding great jobs and setting the world afire. The fire they were setting was obvious in the pile of cigarette butts at their feet where they sat behind a clump of cedar bushes. All four of their eyes were on the door of the 12$^{th}$ Street 7-11.

"As soon as that fat woman comes out and pulls away, we move. Okay?"

Eddie looked at his watch. "It's almost 2:30. Only one car has gone by in the past ten minutes. I'm ready if you are."

"We meet in the park under that little bridge, right? Okay?"

"Yes, for the fiftieth time. Under that little bridge. Just calm down."

"I'm calm," Sanchez shot back. "I'm calm."

Eddie quizzed him one more time. "And which way are you gonna run when you come out the door?"

"To the left."

"That's right. I'll go to the right. Don't slow down or look back. Just run and we'll meet up at the bridge."

Sanchez was feeling a little sick in his stomach. "Say one more time what we do inside?"

"Just follow what I do. Stay right at my elbow. And we both empty the drawer 'cause it's faster if we both do it. Stuff your pockets. Let me take care of the old guy behind the counter."

"You gonna shoot him?"

"Have I ever said I was gonna shoot him?"

"What if he has a gun?"

"I've been in there a thousand times. He don't carry. And his fingers are crooked. Artheritist or whatever you call it.

5

Something like that. I can handle him. You ready? She's pullin' out. Pull your mask up. Let's go."

They ran across the parking lot for the front door. They hit two doors at the same time and began yelling as soon as they were inside.

"Get down! Get down! Get on the floor!"

Herbert Tolly, who was not as old as Sanchez and Eddie thought he was, had been robbed three times before. He knew what to do. As soon as he saw the guns, he went to both knees and then spread himself on the floor behind the counter as far away from the cash register as possible. He didn't want them stepping on him or be close enough they might kick him for no reason at all. He lay still with his face away from the action. By the sound of things, he would guess one of them knew exactly how to open the drawer. It took them only a few seconds. They were scooping the bills out and stuffing their pockets. He could hear them raise the tray and get the fifties he always put underneath.

"Don't get up or you're a dead man. We won't hurt you if you just stay down there."

Herbert never moved or said a word. He just lay as motionless as possible and waited for the sound of the front door opening and closing. When that came, he knew they would be gone. Only a few more seconds and he would raise his head and get up. But then, of course, just as he figured, one of them kicked him in the back for no reason at all and then he heard them running and the doors fanning open. Herbert got to his knees and reached for the phone and dialed 911 as composed as if he were calling home to tell his wife he had to work late. He waited patiently for the 911 operator to answer. Now he could say he had been robbed four times.

Eddie got there first and was sitting under the bridge trying to catch his breath when he saw Sanchez running full speed

# HALF & HALF

toward him. The boy dropped beside his friend and said, "How long you been here?"

"Just now. Did you see anything?"

"Heard a siren."

"I did, too. They will be all over the place in a few minutes so let's split this money up and go home."

Home to Eddie was with an uncle who worked the night shift. His only requirement was that Eddie not make noise while he slept during the day hours. Other than that, Eddie had a free schedule and no one to answer to. Home to Sanchez was with his mother who worried about him constantly but learned years ago she had no control or influence on her son's life or his comings and goings.

"Lay it all out there in a pile and hold that lighter over here and I'll count it out and divvy it up."

Sanchez did as he was told and held the plastic cigarette lighter close to Eddie's face as he counted out $185 to each of them.

"Wow! We did alright," Sanchez almost yelled. "That old guy does a lot a business at night, don't he? One hunnert and eighty-five dollars apiece. What is that all together?"

"Three seventy," Eddie said quickly. "And yeah, that's pretty good for a Thursday night at that 7-11."

"We need to do another one."

"Not too soon," Eddie said. "Let's just head home and let all this cool down. I'll see you somewhere tomorrow."

They both headed across the hill together, splitting at Dauber Street and heading for their respective homes.

Sanchez went in the back door and through the kitchen to his bedroom. He turned on a lamp and smiled at himself in the mirror. He was happy and proud of his night's work and he was anxious to see what his bonus was. He loosened his belt and reached down into his underwear and pulled out $63. Alright. This was the handful of bills he had grabbed from his pockets

7

while he was running and stuffed it away where Eddie couldn't see it. And why not? Everything didn't have to be divided up equally did it?

Eddie used his key to open the front door of his uncle's apartment. He turned on the light in the living room and flopped into the worn recliner. He counted his share one more time and thought to himself that $185 wasn't a bad night's work. Then he pulled his Philly cap off his head and laughed out loud and long as $224 fell down around his shoulders. He couldn't quit laughing.

Yeah, Sanchez and Eddie were best friends. Mainly because no one else wanted to hang with either one of them.

# REVENGE

"I have had it. 1223 is running me ragged."

"Tell me about it. What is it with him, anyway?"

"You know who it is, don't you?"

"Not really. Somebody I should know?"

"Kyle Kingsley. Of Kyle Kingsley Ford."

"Oh, yeah. The car dealer. Can you believe I hadn't even put two and two together? Now I know why I don't like him."

"Nobody does. He's such a jerk."

"Boy, do I know it. He was just layin' on that buzzer a few minutes ago and when I went in he was sittin' up on the edge of his bed, his eyes were blazin' and he jumped all over me like a dog on a dead cat. He said, 'I been ringin' this buzzer for ten minutes and ain't nobody come to see what I want. Is this a hospital or not? What do you nurses do out there? Just drink coffee and gossip?' I told him not to get his gown in a bunch and he didn't like that much at all."

Sharon took another sip of coffee and arched her back to give it a few seconds of stretching. She and Annie laughed about the gown getting in a bunch and then Annie added her story.

"My daughter had a run-in with him about a year ago. She was a waitress at the Rocket Room last summer when she was off from college. Kingsley and his party came in one night for dinner. It was about eight of them I think. They all ordered up big and it was a Saturday night. Place was packed and running over and my daughter said it did take a little longer than usual to get the orders to the tables. So when they got ready to leave, Kingsley and his party, and she brought their bill to lay it on the table, he made a real big deal out of it. She said he got real loud and said, 'Little lady, I just want you to know that I am a good tipper. A big tipper. But tonight you and this restaurant ain't deserving of my tips. So here you go. I'm gonna give you a dollar because that's all your service was worth.' And he actually handed her a dollar bill right in front of everybody. She said all the people at his table just kind of looked at the floor. They were as embarrassed as my daughter was. Jerk!"

Sharon just shook her head and said, "That is so low."

The two night nurses were joined by a third who walked up just as the story was finished.

"And who are you girls talking about?"

"1223," Annie said.

"Oh, my lord. Oh, my lord. Kyle Kingsley. That man is…well, I don't want to say what he is."

"You've had trouble with him, too?" Sharon asked.

"My husband and I bought a car from him once and he was the nastiest and rudest man I have ever been around. He did everything but feel me up in his office while Kevin was signing the papers. He is one total dud."

"I've never heard anybody say anything good about him," Sharon said. "Annie will have to tell you the story she just told me about what he did to her daughter. That is as crappy a thing as I have ever heard of in my life. Oh, the board's lightin' up at my end of the hall. See you girls later." And Sharon was off.

"I want to hear that story, Annie, but right now I have to go to his room to give him 60 milligrams of Oxycodone. I know what he is but he really is in a lot of pain."

Annie reached for the paper cup in her fellow nurse's hand and said, "I'll take it to him. I'm going that way anyhow. I have to get a stack of linens from the closet down there."

Annie walked the semi-dark corridor passing room after room with their doors slightly ajar. She could see all the rooms were dark except for the one she was approaching. Light was shining from under the closed door that read #1223 and she could hear moaning coming from inside. But it wasn't Kyle Kingsley that was prominent in her mind at the moment. It was her daughter and the tears of humiliation and embarrassment

## HALF & HALF

she had cried that night last summer when she got home. Annie was about to push on the door handle and walk in with the instant pain relief in her hand when her toe lightly stumped a trash receptacle. She stopped and looked down at the swinging top on the blue trashcan. Who would know? A dollar? Really, a dollar?

Nobody would know, big tipper. Nobody.

# HOME

The sign on the interstate said LEXINGTON, VA 23 MILES. Seven-year-old Sara Bensen was asleep in the backseat of the two-year-old Lexus. Her mother, Audrey, was staring silently out the windshield from the front passenger seat. Her father, Gary, was driving the speed limit and glancing intermittently at his wife as the passing cars flashed their headlights across her face. The radio between them was playing something from the 60s that neither one of them recognized and was barely listening to anyway.

"Did you see that sign?" he asked.

Audrey didn't answer. He wasn't sure if she was ignoring him or actually didn't hear him. He asked again.

"I saw it. And I heard you the first time."

"Then why didn't you answer me?"

"Because I know what your next question is going to be and I don't want to have this conversation."

"Hey, we don't have to…"

"I know," she interrupted. "I know you're trying to do the right thing and it's me. It's all on me. And I don't know what to do."

"Oh, I think you know what you should…"

"Yeah, okay. I know what I should do but I also know what I want to do and they are not the same thing. No matter how hard I try to make it come out, they are not the same thing."

Gary turned the radio down and glanced in the backseat to make sure they had not wakened their daughter. She was still snug in the blankets they had piled around her so she could sleep through as much of the night as possible. They had left their house in Harrisburg, PA after he got off from work this evening and were headed to Sarasota, FL to vacation at his parents' house for the next ten days. He hoped to make it to Charlotte

# HALF & HALF

before they checked in for a few hours' sleep. Unless Audrey decided to stop in Lexington. He couldn't read her for sure and wanted to make certain she didn't do something she may regret come morning. He spoke softly to her trying to show no signs of coaxing.

"I know the last time you saw her was at your mother's funeral three years ago. That's a long time for sisters to go without seeing one another. Especially sisters as close as you were at one time."

Silence filled the car except for the faint sound of The Supremes singing something about 'being together.' He let his last sentence linger to see if she would pick it up or not. She did.

"Growing up we could not have been closer. Only a year and a half difference in our ages. We wore the same clothes; always the same size. We played the same sports. Even dated the same boys a couple of times. We were more like twins than just sisters. And I guess I miss her. I won't lie to you."

"And don't you think she misses you?"

"I honestly don't know. I swear to you I don't know."

"When was the last time you talked to her?"

"It was on the phone."

"I know it was on the phone. But when? How long ago?"

"We've talked twice since Mamma died. I called *her* both times. The first time was two weeks after the funeral. That's when she told me she and Martin were moving into Mamma's house. Never asked me if it was okay being as how half of the house is mine. No. Never mind about that. She and Martin, that unemployed bum she's shacked up with, she and Martin are moving into our Mamma and Daddy's house. The house we grew up in. Martin will be sleeping and eating in our house. In our home. Damn it, Gary. I'm sorry but I can't stand it.

"I know. Don't get upset."

LEXINGTON, VA 11 MILES.

Don Reid

She reached over and took his hand in hers and just held it. She wanted to say something more but didn't know if she could say anything more without crying. Then she checked over her shoulder to make sure Sara was still asleep.

"When was the second time?"

"What?"

"When was the second time you called her?"

"That first Christmas. I told you about that."

"I know you did but you need to tell me again. You need to talk about it as much as possible in the next ten minutes because we are coming up on the Lexington exit and you have got to decide if we're going to take it or not. So tell me about the second time you called her."

"You were there. It was Christmas morning. The first Christmas after Mamma had passed away and I called like I always did. And *he* answered the phone. That lazy, no-good Martin Stone answered the phone and told me my sister was busy and could I call back at a more 'convenient time.' Why did she ever hook up with that scum? He hasn't worked in five years. He looks bad. He smells bad. And I know he beats her."

"You don't know that."

"I know it, Gary. Trust me. I know it. I can tell. We can tell things between us. I could tell the last time I saw Shirley just how miserable she was without her telling me anything at all. I know. Believe me, I know."

"You've got two more miles. Do we take the exit or not. We can stay as long or leave as soon as you want. It's up to you. It has to be your decision."

Gary turned the radio completely off and there was nothing to be heard in the car except thick silence.

"Audrey, we're a hundred yards from the exit. Tell me what you want to do."

14

# HALF & HALF

"I don't know if I'm ready to see Martin Stone living in my childhood home. Just thinking about it makes me almost throw up."

Putting on the brakes, Gary said one last time, "Fifty feet to the exit."

Audrey sighed a heavy sigh and said with tears in her eyes, "Maybe we'll stop next week on the way back."

# DEBT

Jack sat behind his grandfather's desk where he never thought he would ever sit. The job was already daunting and he hadn't even gotten started. Being the only male grandchild, it had all fallen in his lap. His older sister was not going to spend her time going through the personal papers and boxes. She had already told him to just toss the contents and move on. Oh, Ann had loved her grandfather but she just wasn't the sentimental type. Jack was just the opposite. He couldn't throw away a yellowed envelope or a small box with rubber bands around it without looking into what each item was and reading each note. Truth be known, it was fun for him and he was learning more about Grand Pop as each old desk drawer was cleaned out. He had only been gone a month and the memories were still very tender as Jack went through the final cache in the back of one of the lower drawers.

There were old pictures of people he didn't know and his grandmother's mind was in no condition to help him identify them. There were some hand-written notes in a faded pencil scrawl he could ask his dad about but he was of the same mind as Ann, so he had quit bothering him with questions weeks ago. But the one that had caught his attention with the greatest interest was a small, sealed, unwrinkled envelope marked DEBT. He had laid it aside early this morning, but now as he was putting everything in either the trash or a keepsake box, he reached for it. Turning it over to slit the side of it, he noticed a dated message on the back:

APRIL 26, 1957     $100   BET      BUB HAMILTON

He opened it and found a small piece of paper inside with a few words in the same fading, pencil scrawl that was now growing so familiar to his eyes. All of this brought a slight shiver to his spine. He could feel a mystery growing and knew that he

# HALF & HALF

would do all he could to find out what the cryptic $100 debt was. He held it in his hand and smiled as he read the envelope time and again.

Bub Hamilton was a big man in town. He had been a state senator most of his life and owned a chain of breweries and bottling companies all over the state. He had heard Grand Pop say a number of times that they had been friends in their earlier lives, but he wasn't mentioned much in later years. Jack had met Bub Hamilton on a few occasions and knew some of the Hamilton family socially. He smiled to himself thinking about this envelope and note and wondered if the old man would find it amusing to be reminded of something this ancient and probably this unimportant. Why not? All the stories he had heard about Bub Hamilton had not been pretty. He was a crotchety and sarcastic old codger who seldom had a kind word or a gentle thought for anyone. But what harm could be done? He picked up the phone book and made a couple of calls that led to an appointment with the rich old legend the following Monday afternoon.

Richard T. "Bub" Hamilton was sitting in his downtown office behind his mahogany desk, resplendent in a gray suit, matching gray tie and white starched shirt. He looked neither retired nor anywhere close to his 77 years of age even though he was both. A stooped, elderly secretary who didn't bother to rise, invited Jack to "go on in." Bub stood and greeted him.

"Well, for God's sakes. You look just like your granddaddy Jack. And they call you Jack, too?"

"That's right, sir," Jack said as the old man grasped and squeezed his hand.

"Sit down, boy. Sit down. What in the world have you got on your mind today?"

Jack noted to himself that even though he was being good-ole-boyed and charmed in a loud voice, the royal Mr.

Hamilton made little small talk. He got right to the point letting Jack know that the whole afternoon was not his.

"Well, sir, as you probably know, my grandfather, Jack Wilmington, passed away about a month ago."

"I sure did know that. I sent your family flowers. Sorry I wasn't able to get there myself, but I liked old Jack. Good man. Good friend."

"Well," Jack continued, "I've been going through a lot of my grandfather's things. I was cleaning out his desk the other day and found something with your name on it. It was dated nearly 60 years ago."

"Sixty years ago?" Bub Hamilton interrupted. "Sixty years ago we were in college at UVA in Charlottesville, Virginia. You know Charlottesville?"

"Oh, yes sir. Quite well."

"Thirteenth largest city in the state of Virginia. Not too big. Not too small. Just a good-sized town that's got everything you need but not too much of it. You know what I mean?"

"Yes, sir. I think I do. Anyhow, I found this envelope with the date of April 26, 1957 on it."

"1957? My God, boy, that was nearly 60 years ago."

"Yes sir. And it had your name on it."

"And my address?"

"No address. It just said DEBT on it. Then it said just your name and beside your name was written $100 BET. Does this ring any kind of bell in your memory?"

Old Bub looked a long time at young Jack without saying a word. It wasn't as long as a minute but it felt like an hour. He changed positions in his chair and looked at his desk for another long moment and finally said, "Why do you ask?"

"No specific reason, Mr. Hamilton. I was just curious. I'm kind of a history nut and I love old papers and artifacts and I guess you can say I'm a sucker for a little mystery. No big deal. I just thought it would be interesting to find out what Grand Pop

Jack meant by this little obscure note in the back of one of his desk drawers."

"I tell you what, Jack. I do remember that note but what it means is really none of your business but I can appreciate you wanting to know about it. I found a letter in an old book I had bought at an auction one time. I read somebody's thoughts from a century before and my imagination would just send me on the wildest of dreams every time I read that thing over and over. I wonder where it is today. Since Estelle died three years ago, I've lost track of things like that. I wouldn't even know where to start looking for that letter or even that book, for that matter."

"I know it's none of my business," Jack began as he was again interrupted by his host.

"I shouldn't have said it like that. I didn't mean anything by it. I was just saying...I tell you what, son. Close that door there."

Jack got up and quietly closed the door that led to the secretary's office and promptly resumed his position in the chair in front of Bub Hamilton's desk.

"I've never told anybody this story and I'd just as soon you didn't either. We were young, your granddaddy and me. Probably junior year at Virginia. What year did you say?"

"1957."

"Yes, junior year. Second semester. We hung out together all the time. Went to all the parties and dated all the girls. Not much got by either one of us if you know what I mean, Jack. Well, there was this beautiful girl we spotted one morning working in the cafeteria. She was a student and I have to tell you she had the prettiest face I had ever seen in my life. Dark eyes, perfect mouth, pearl-white teeth and hair down to her shoulders. We both saw her at the same time. And we both came back there about every morning from then on to look at her again and to occasionally talk to her. And that's when we made our bet. We bet each other $100 to see which one of us

19

Don Reid

would date and bed this beauty first. We agreed to stop coming to the cafeteria together. We were each on our own and we had to be honest with one another. And the winner had to bring proof that he had won. We didn't say what it had to be but we knew what we were talking about. One hundred dollars.

So your granddaddy was the first to get a date with her. He took her to the movies one night. Two nights later, I took her to a lecture on campus. Some popular writer was there. I think it was Kerouac or one of those beatnik guys. And then Jack took her out one more time I think and then me and then that was it. She and I fell in love and got married six months later and were married for 55 years. Estelle Freeman. The love of my life. She passed three years ago this June. It was years before I told her that Jack Wilmington and I had a bet on about her. She just laughed and laughed when I told her. What a woman. I love her more today than I did even then. But now, son, you have to keep this story to yourself. It sort of makes me look bad. Gambling for the woman of my dreams like that. But it all turned out good."

"I promise you, sir, your secret is safe with me. I was just curious about it all."

"Of course, you were. No problem, son. Don't know why Jack kept it as a reminder that he had lost a $100 bet. You don't want to pay it for him do you, boy?"

"No sir, I sure don't. But I certainly thank you for your time today."

A few more minutes of pleasantries were exchanged and Jack eventually saw himself out of the office. Walking to the parking lot he reached in his pocket and looked one more time at the envelope that read DEBT. APRIL 26, 1957. $100 BET. BUB HAMILTON. Then he reached inside the envelope and pulled out the small piece of paper in the fading scrawl and read it to himself one more time. *Bub Hamilton owes me $100.*

20

# HALF & HALF

Jack crumpled the note and envelope and threw them into the nearest trashcan.

# MURDER

David Carson sat in the dark, silent house and looked out the upstairs window. It was the 36th night in a row he had been alone in this bedroom. The loneliness was eating into him so deeply he wasn't even sure what day it was. He did remember vividly it was a Sunday afternoon that she left. She had packed quickly and without fanfare. With no exchange of any words, she had put her three pink pieces of luggage in the Toyota and driven out the lane. The note was on the countertop in the kitchen:

*This is it. I've tried so many times before but this time I am gone. We have no secrets. I will be at Ron's house. If you need to get in touch with me, call him. But only if it is an emergency. And please don't try to contact me at work. That would only be awkward for both of us.    --Denise*

He had read the note at least 50 times but when he finally decided what he was going to do, he tossed it the trashcan under the sink. He would put it all in motion tomorrow morning.

Ron Justice lived on a county road about six miles out of town. David knew he and Denise would both be at work so he planned to arrive there by 10 a.m. just to be safe. He parked his car in the driveway beside the house and stood for a moment or two just to make sure there was no one at home. He couldn't see or feel any movement and there was very little traffic on the road for anyone to spot his car. But that possibility was certainly reason enough to act as quickly as he could. He walked to the door on the side of the garage and pushed it open. It was empty of any vehicles and smelled of oil and rubber. The cement floor was stained with spots of leaking fluids and the garbage can was overflowing a bit, but it looked like anyone's normal garage. He honestly didn't know what he was looking for but he was sure he would know it when he saw it. And there it was in the corner. Two softball gloves, a pair of cleats and two bats. This would do nicely. He pulled a pair of plastic gloves from his hip pocket, put them on his hands and picked up one of the bats. He stopped at a tool bin and looked inside it. He opened all the drawers under the workbench. There he found three pairs of oily work gloves in varied worn condition. He picked out the worst looking pair as he figured these would be the ones least likely to be missed and carried them in the same hand with the softball bat. He closed the door of the garage behind him as he went out. He put the bat and the gloves in the trunk of his car, looked around for any oncoming traffic, and seeing none, took the plastic gloves off, and threw them in the passenger seat as he got in his car and pulled off.

David smiled to himself as he drove back to town. How long would it take to miss a ball bat in the middle of winter? Months. This was even more perfect than he had imagined.

David had heard from a few different friends that Ron Justice and Denise went to eat at the Hansford Bar and Grille often. Someone had even said they were there three or four times a week around dinnertime and would stay for sometimes three or four hours for drinks. Not having any idea when he might catch them there, his only hope was to make himself a regular so as not to miss them. So starting that Monday evening, he began popping in for dinner around six o'clock. He took his time eating and ordered a few drinks and found he rather enjoyed the people and the atmosphere. It wasn't until Thursday at 6:10 p.m. that the confrontation he had been waiting for took place. He had just ordered dinner when his wife and Ron Justice walked in the door hand-in-hand. Denise was the first to spot David and she stopped so quickly it almost threw both of them off balance. She whispered something in Ron's ear and together they proceeded to the farthest table in the corner. A few other

# Don Reid

customers came in and were seated and it was all going just the way David had hoped for. Even seeing Ron finally get out of his seat and approach his table, it was all David could do to suppress a smile.

Ron spoke first and loudly. "What are you doing here?"

"Eating dinner."

"Yeah, but why here?"

"Because this is where they serve food?"

"You've got a smart mouth, Carson. And I don't like your attitude. And I don't like you being here."

"Where would you like for me to be?" David asked and almost sounded sincere.

"You know this is where Denise and I come."

"I had no idea where you come or go or what you do."

"Listen, Carson, don't follow us. Or you'll be sorry you did."

"What's that?" David asked as the room got totally quiet and all the customers sat looking into their laps but listening intently.

Ron Justice clinched his teeth and said in a voice louder than he meant to, "You follow us here or anywhere else and you'll be sorry. Trust me, you will be sorry."

A waitress arrived with David's Ruben sandwich and stepped in front of Ron as she placed it on the table. Simultaneously with the delivery of the sandwich, the manager walked up to the table and said, "Is there a problem here?"

David replied politely, "No sir," while Ron Justice turned and walked back to his table without saying another word.

David ate slowly as the room came back up to its normal pitch. Denise and Ron never looked his way again. Even as he got up fifteen minutes later, paid his bill and walked out.

There was only one more step and then this chapter in his life would be over. He sat and rubbed his forehead and closed his eyes to be sure he had covered every base. He could think of

24

no loose ends. No stumbling block. No hole the police could find in the story. Everything would prove itself. He had been practicing her handwriting and he felt he had it mastered at last. That little rushed and broken way she attacked each word. The small sometimes half printing mixed in with a cursive style that was all her own. He sat now and practiced it some more. He was ready to do the final masterpiece and then he would place it on the steering wheel of Ron's truck just before he got off from work. Ron would come out to the parking lot and find it and go into a rage. He knew Ron so well. It was the only advantage in having your once best friend as your current archenemy. He would come barreling into David's driveway and David would be ready for him.

He pulled alongside Ron's pickup. It was never locked so this would be a cinch. He opened the door and stuck the note where it would be seen immediately. Right in front of his eyes. He looked all around the parking lot and made sure no one had seen him. Then he eased back into his car and glanced through the truck window one more time at the note.

Ron,
Come to David's house and fast. Don't bother to try to call me.
He has taken my phone. Things are about to blow.
I need you there as soon as you can get there. Please hurry.
Love you,
D

Ron Justice's blue truck came up David's driveway and took the final turn on two wheels. He jumped out of it so fast he didn't even bother to close the door. David heard him banging on the backdoor with both hands. He calmly went to the door and opened it.

"Where is she, David? What's going on here?" Ron said through clenched teeth.

"Come on in, Ron. She's in the kitchen."

## Don Reid

Ron stormed through the kitchen and stopped in the middle of the room. He looked at David with an angry and puzzled look.

"I don't see her. Where is she?"

"It's all over, Ron, old pal of mine. It's all over."

And at this, David pulled the trigger on his .45 caliber pistol and shot Ron cleanly through the heart. With the plastic gloves on that Ron had not even noticed, David picked up the softball bat from the corner of the kitchen and walked out the backdoor. He used the big end of the bat to break out a window panel closest to the doorknob. He walked back in and closed the door behind him. He dropped the bat on the floor beside Ron's freshly dead body and then put the old worn work gloves on each of Ron's hands. This would cover any reason why no finger prints at all could be found on the inside backdoor lock. He would tell how he was upstairs and heard the speeding truck come up his driveway (and he liked the added touch of the driver's door still hanging open). He heard breaking glass so he grabbed his pistol from a desk drawer and found Ron Justice in his kitchen. He took a swing at him with a ball bat he had apparently brought from home and to protect himself, David shot him. An intruder who was trying to do him danger. Any number of people at the Hansford Bar and Grille could attest to Ron's anger toward him; even the manager and one of the waiting staff. The only thing left to do was find that note. It was probably in the truck seat or in one of Ron's pockets. And then call the police and report a home invasion. Self-defense inside his house? No cop, judge or jury would even think of calling this murder.

David smiled to himself and dialed the phone.

# COURAGE

It was Janie's first day of school. A day she had dreamed about and looked forward to from as far back as she could remember. She walked the two blocks from her house to the old stately school building alone. It grew so much bigger the closer she got to it. She didn't know exactly what to expect or what would be expected of her. She had carried that tight, anxious feeling in the bottom of her stomach from the minute she awoke this morning. She would have backed out at the very last minute if she thought she could have gotten away with it. But her mother had sensed her reluctance and had encouraged her all the more. She had kissed her on the cheek and given her a hug and calmed her nerves as only a mother can do.

Her imaginations were mounting. As the Thomas A. Edison Elementary school came firmly in front of her, she found herself standing in a frozen position, staring at its intimidating size. Excitement rushed through her. She was sure she would like it. She may even find a friend who lived in her direction and could walk to and from school with her each day.

She climbed the cement steps and walked through the opened doorway. At the second door, she pushed hard on the long brass handle. Would it always be this heavy and this hard to open? Then the huge door slammed shut behind her, echoing through the hollow corridors. The serious gloom of the walls and the school smell immediately brought back the nervous stomach. That mysterious trace of chalk, books and mustiness that the summer brought about, permeated throughout the hallways and rooms. It is something that will be with schools as long as they are built of wood, cinderblock and red brick.

She was actually beginning to be afraid now. And she noted the frightened look on all the faces of the children around her. The little girl in the blue dress with the red eyes who apparently had been crying all morning. The little boy in the ball cap with the runny nose who was too embarrassed to blow because of the noise it would make. And, oh, the little blonde-haired boy on the front row who sat stiffly with his jacket zipped up to his chin because he was too bashful to turn and face the class and make that long walk to the coat closet in the back of the room.

Janie smiled to herself. Why should she be frightened? Everyone was frightened and they would all begin their first day of school together. She laughed, almost out loud and took her seat at the desk at the front of the room. And then she called the class to order.

# COWBOY

Keith Derrick stopped his dusty Ford pickup near the front steps of the building. He sat for a moment to gather his thoughts and to get his 6-foot 2-inch sore body into gear to gracefully exit the dented and rusted vehicle he had called his for nearly nine years. It was time to trade up and get out of his chosen life and this meeting just might be the solution to both of those goals. His knees and ankles ached and cracked as he stepped down to the hot pavement of the parking lot. He had to stand for a moment in his cowboy boots, with the slanted riding heel, to get his spine ready to negotiate those concrete steps to the front door of Arthur Masincup's office.

The sign on the door carried the name and trademark of the National Rodeo Association. He had been here before but this was the first time he had been called here. He wasn't sure what Arthur wanted with him but he had a few hours before he had to leave on the next tour and Arthur had always been a good friend to him. He hoisted his 38-year-old body up the stairs, feeling a new pain with each excruciating lifting of his legs. How did a man this young get in such a shape he asked himself. The answer was obviously bull riding and broncos but he was reluctant to accept this even from himself. Surely, there were a few more good years left if he could get past the daily aches. As he opened the front door, he could see into Masincup's inter office. He motioned for Keith to come on back.

Arthur Masincup booked practically every rodeo in Texas, Oklahoma and New Mexico. He set all the big ones such as the Santa Fe Days, Frontier Days in Cheyenne and the Stampede in Calgary. He even set regular dates on the east coast and in the Midwest where rodeo was always a sure draw. And he did it all year round from this desk and this small office in Austin. Arthur was an unlikely looking cowboy promoter. He stood five inches

29

shy of six-feet, was bald as a brass doorknob, and wore a pencil-thin mustache that must take ten minutes to trim every morning. He watched Keith as he folded into the chair opposite his desk and listened to him groan and sigh like a man twice his age before he spoke.

"You sound like you're 80 years old. Why do you let yourself get in that shape?"

Keith smiled and said, "Don't have much choice, Mr. A. That's what cowboys do. We get throwed in the dirt. People like to see it. That's what pays the bills."

"Well, I have a new deal for you. You'll never get thrown on your face again and have to eat that arena mud and whatever else is mixed in there with it." Arthur laughed to himself at his clever phrasing. "I need a new advance man. Paul Potter is retiring and I need someone who already knows the ropes and who won't be retiring on me in a few years. You interested?"

Keith was interested. He had all the trophies he ever wanted. He had saved very little money but practically owned a small ranch style house just outside of town. Yes, he could honestly say he was interested.

"I am. What you got in mind?"

"You go ahead of the rodeos about two weeks. All the advertisement is bought by computer or phone, but I need a flesh and bone guy there before the show gets into town. You meet with the newspapers, the radio stations, some merchants. You give away some tickets. You make sure everything is in place before the livestock and setup guys pull into town. You're kind of a face of trust and respectability for the money people to see. You shake hands and put out fires. You got me?"

"Sure. I can do that. What kind of money?"

"A weekly salary. We'll work all of that out. Don't worry about it. You'll like it. Lots of places you can drive. I'll cover your expenses. Sometimes you'll have to fly. And, it'll beat limping around like an old cripple at your young age. This will be a good job for you."

"Mr. A. I really appreciate you thinking of me. I love the idea of getting off those horses. I think I could like this a lot. Thank you so much for the opportunity. When do I start?"

"In two weeks. That'll give you a chance to meet with Potter a few times and, ah yeah, get you some clothes."

"What do you mean, sir?"

"Some clothes, boy. Some business clothes. I'd be willing to bet you ain't got a decent suit of clothes. I've seen you riders go to funerals and weddings in those jeans and plaid shirts. You need some clothes. Do you even own a suit?"

"No, sir. I don't have the need."

"Well, you do now," Arthur shot back.

"What do you mean, Mr. A.?"

"I mean a pair of dress pants. A sport coat. Something decent to wear when you walk into a man's office in whatever city you may be in."

"A tie?" Keith asked with a look of pain on his suntanned face.

"A tie is optional but an open-collar shirt, a white one or even a blue one. Something solid. Can you handle that, son?"

"Yes, sir, I think I can. And I'll be ready to start any day you say."

Keith pushed his body out of his seat with both hands on the chair arms and stood, arching his back to relieve the constant pain. He shook hands with Arthur Mansincup who assured him he would phone him in the next 24 hours with a game plan. Keith opened the door behind him and was about to exit when Arthur offered one more parting suggestion.

"And some loafers."

"What's that, sir?"

"Some loafers. You know, shoes. Get a pair of shoes. Oxfords. Something business like."

31

# Don Reid

"You mean something besides cowboy boots, Mr. A.?"

"Yeah, Keith. Something besides cowboy boots. You'll be dealing with business men with suits and polished shoes."

Keith Derrick stood a long moment and stared at nothing in particular; then at Arthur Masincup's bald head; then at his own scarred and scuffed boots with the slanted riding heel. He wasn't sure how to say it and he knew it would be best left unsaid but he might as well take care of the situation now than later.

"Well, thanks anyway, Arthur. I appreciate the offer but I guess I'd rather eat arena mud and *whatever else is mixed in there with it.*"

Keith slammed the door behind him and limped his way out to his old dusty Ford pickup.

# CHERRY

Russell Bainbridge stood at the front office window of Handels Funeral Home, looking out into the parking lot. He was waiting for his eleven o'clock appointment and they were just getting out of the white Chrysler van.

"The Conyer party is here," he said to his receptionist/secretary sitting at her desk.

"You know none of them is a Conyer, don't you?" Mattie asked without looking up.

"Yes. I think they are nieces and a nephew. Right?" Russell Bainbridge asked without taking his eyes off the three middle-aged people who all bore a strong family resemblance.

"The deceased never had children," Mattie said, as she joined her boss at the window. "I guess it has fallen to these three to take care of their uncle's funeral. And they should with the money he's probably leaving them. I know all three of them. Have for years. That's Maynard Strickler getting out from under the wheel. He's never kept a job for over a year in his entire life. He's not worth running over. He's the one you'll have the most problem with. And there, getting out on the other side, that's his sister Katherine Mines. She's married to Harvey Mines from Hamilton Falls. You know him."

"I know of him," Russell Bainbridge interjected.

"Well, she's the boss of all of them. They will go with whatever she says in the long run so she's the one you will really have to deal with. And there, getting out of the back seat, that's Alma. She's the sweetest of them all. Never married and is very active in her church. Lutheran. She runs the family business and has ever since their daddy died."

"What was the family business?" Russell asked, as he had only lived in the area a few years and Mattie was a native.

33

# Don Reid

"Paving. Blue Devil Paving. Strange business for a woman to run but Maynard was never any help. I don't imagine she would hire him to drive one of the trucks."

Russell Bainbridge walked to the front door, opened it and welcomed his customers to the necessary but unfortunate duty for which they had come.

The meeting and conversation eventually led to the Casket Room or the Show Room or the Sales Floor. Whatever you called it, it was the place no one wanted to enter or stay too long. It was a large, oblong room filled with at least a dozen caskets and burial encasements. Russell Bainbridge's voice lowered and took on a tone of reverence as soon as they entered this chamber. All three of Berle Conyer's family members became strangely quiet and uncomfortable as they looked around the room at their next turn of duty. Russell Bainbridge spoke first.

"Choosing a casket is a very important part of your experience today. You want something that will be durable and protective and even attractive. We have a large price range represented here as you can see and I will be glad to answer any question you may have about any of them."

"How much is this one?" Maynard asked pointing at the one nearest to where he was standing.

"That is our Titan. It's made of 20-guage steel and is very practical."

"But how much is it?" Maynard asked again.

"That sells for eight ninety-five."

"Eight hundred and ninety-five dollars?" Maynard asked in disbelief.

"Yes, sir," Russell Bainbridge answered in his best mortuary voice.

"Is there something cheaper?" Maynard asked with no shame.

34

# HALF & HALF

"Maynard, stop it," Katherine scolded. "We're not here to get Uncle Berle the cheapest of the lot."

"Well, we're paying for it, ain't we?" Maynard shot back. "I mean Aunt Cookie ain't able to do this and whatever we save her now, we'll get more later. That's the way I look at it."

Embarrassed, Alma addressed Russell Bainbridge and said, "Our aunt, Mr. Conyer's widow, is in a nursing home. While she doesn't have complete dementia, she does suffer from severe abulia and that is why we have taken charge of all the funeral arrangements. You will meet Aunt Cookie Wednesday night at the Visitation, if indeed she is able to come."

Before Russell could acknowledge Alma's explanation, Katherine said from deeper in the room, "Oh, this is nice. What is this Mr. Bainbridge?"

"That is very nice. That's our top of the line. That is called the Venetian. It is solid Cherry Hardwood. Very nice," he said as he ran his hand over the deep colored, sleek wood.

"How much is that one?" Maynard piped in.

"That one would run you in the neighborhood of thirty-nine hundred dollars."

"Four thousand dollars?" Maynard nearly yelled. "Are you kidding me? And that other one, that steel one is eight ninety-five? That's over three thousand dollars difference. We'll take the steel one."

"We will not, Maynard," and this time it was sister Alma quieting him. "We may look at something more in the mid-range, but we will not get Uncle Berle the cheapest box in the house. He meant more to me than that and should mean more to you."

"Yeah, and why? What did he ever do for you that was so special? He took us to the beach one summer when we were kids and stayed drunk the whole week. And that's worth three thousand dollars to me?"

35

Don Reid

Oblivious to any other conversation, Katherine said again, as if only to herself, "I certainly do love this Cherry. Aunt Cookie has a chest of drawers almost identical to this. I just know this is what she would choose."

Trying to keep peace and move the sale along, Russell Bainbridge spoke to anyone who might want to listen, "And we do have something in between. This is a Spruce and 18-guage casket and it sells for twenty-four hundred."

"We'll take the eight ninety-five one," Maynard said with authority.

"We will not," Alma said shortly, getting red in the face.

Katherine from the back of the room offered, "This Cherry is what I would pick for myself and I think Uncle Berle would be happy with it, too."

"I suggest we vote," Alma offered.

"Okay with me," Maynard said quickly. "I vote for the steel one. Eight hundred and ninety five smackers. And stick a bottle of Bud inside it for Uncle Berle's trip."

"Maynard, you are awful," Katherine said. "I vote for the Cherry. It is so beautiful."

They both looked to their sister Alma for the final and deciding vote. She studied all three choices and ran her hand over each one trying hard to muster up fairness and good taste.

"I know we will benefit in the end, as Maynard has pointed out, if we try to save Aunt Cookie's money, but I also know she would want the best for him. He wasn't always the warmest and most loving uncle in the world and he often was nasty to our daddy, who was the kindest and sweetest man who ever lived. Uncle Berle had a temper and wasn't shy about showing it but he also had a soft spot for his animals. Remember those little bull dogs he always had? As soon as one would die, he would get another one. Buster, Beanie, and Bo-Bo. He wasn't always a good man, but he was decent and good to Aunt Cookie and she loved him. Considering everything, I guess I will have to vote

36

for…oh, heavens, I could go either way now that I think about it. But I guess I will vote for the Cherry."

"Bless you," said Katherine.

"Damn," said Maynard.

"Sold," said Russell Bainbridge.

# LUNCH

Ralph and Glenn had come to the Blue Stone every Tuesday for lunch for the past twenty-three years. They always sat at the same table and if on chance someone was already seated at said table, they would patiently wait on the bench by the cashier's desk until it became open. The table was by the window because Ralph tended to become nervous when he couldn't see if the weather was changing while they sat, ate and talked for easily two and a half hours each week. Juanita had only been their waitress for a decade of their reign at table number three, but she had come to know them well and to love them for the elderly gentlemen they had grown into.

Ralph Garman had owned and managed a supermarket for forty-one years. He finally gave into the chain stores, sold out and retired comfortably with great expectations of moving to Florida and spending the rest of his life fishing and sailing. Life, though, taught Ralph a few lessons about who was in charge when his sweet and loving wife, Ellen, passed away just months after his employees had given him that beautiful gold watch. He never made it to the shores and riverbanks of the Sunshine State and graciously retired his dreams to the home he had shared with Ellen for so many wonderful years. He joined a few civic clubs, visited his grown children and grandkids in a neighboring state each Easter and Christmas, and basically, found the peace and comfort that goes with a lessened schedule and aging joints. He wasn't particularly happy but he wasn't unhappy. And maybe that was all one should expect from life after all.

Glenn Farley had kept books for practically everyone in town. All of his career, he maintained an office over a local barbershop and even held on to the lease for a couple of years after he decided to hang it all up. He enjoyed going to his desk and just looking down on Main Street the way he had grown

38

# HALF & HALF

accustomed to doing all those years in business. But he grew so tired of having so little to do that he cleaned out his files, carried them to the local landfill and even threw his framed CPA license onto the smoldering pile of garbage before he drove away. He knew this would seal his retirement and he would never be tempted to ever go back to work no matter how bored he might become. He had no wife to spend the money he had saved. She had left decades ago. His house was long paid for and only nieces and nephews stood to inherit from him. His life was simple and just about the only regular event he had to look forward to each week was that Tuesday lunch date with his old friend and confidant.

Glenn and Ralph knew each other's secrets and could finish each other's sentences. Two old compadres in their late, declining eighties, helping one another to and from their chairs was an endearing sight to anyone who cared to watch and learn what friendship and caring was all about. The Blue Stone was their refuge and their third party in these weekly visits. They never once considered having lunch at any other establishment. It was always the same table and the same order. Juanita knew without asking that Ralph would have the hamburger steak, mashed potatoes and a fried egg. Glenn would, without waver, have the meatloaf with fried apples and snow peas. Sweet teas for them both would be the order of the day and the tip was always a respectable eighteen per cent. But Juanita was shocked as she rounded the corner from the kitchen on this particular Tuesday at midday and saw Ralph sitting alone at his and Glenn's designated table.

"Mr. Garman. Good afternoon."

"Hello, Juanita," Ralph said looking up into her familiar face while hanging his cane on the back of his chair. "How are you today, honey?"

"I'm doing just fine. Where's your partner in crime? He on his way?"

# Don Reid

"No, sweetheart, he won't be here today."

"Oh, my goodness. I hope he's not sick."

"No he's not sick. But he won't be here today or ever again."

"Oh, my God. What do you mean?"

"Gone."

"He's gone? Mr. Farley's gone?"

"Yep. Last Thursday night about 7:30."

Juanita sat down heavily in the chair opposite her customer. She had never before done this at any table or wait station in her life, but suddenly her legs would not hold her. She looked directly into Ralph Garman's face and reached for one of his hands.

"Please don't tell me Mr. Farley is…"

"Gone," Ralph finished her sentence. "Gone to Kentucky. I put him on the train last Thursday night at 7:30. I'm sending his clothes and furniture out that way sometime later this week. As soon as I can get some folks together to help me pack it all up."

"Oh, Mr. Garman. You had me scared to death. When you said he was gone, I mean, I thought you meant… really gone."

"No, No," Ralph chuckled. "Just moved to another state."

"For good?"

"Oh, yes, for good. We'll probably never see him again. It was pretty quick. One day he was here and the next he was up and gone."

Juanita took a moment to get her breath back and said, "Has he gone to live with family?"

Ralph shook his head. "He's got no family. Just him. 'Course now I guess he's got some family where he's going."

"What do you mean?" Juanita asked.

Ralph laughed to himself, rubbed his day-old stubble of whiskers and said, "Glenn got himself married."

40

# HALF & HALF

"Married? At his age?" Juanita hated herself immediately for that last question but knew it was too late to retract it.

"Exactly," Ralph said with a grin. "He met this woman on the internet he said. I don't mess with all that stuff but Glenn did. And he said they fell in love. She owned a house out there around Lexington someplace and before I knew who shot Joe, he just up and moved. Asked me to take him to the train, so I did. It was kinda sad to see him leave but I can understand it. There wasn't anything keeping him here. His wife left him years and years ago and I'm sure he'll be happy out there. Glenn always liked horses and that's horse country, you know."

"Well, I sure am sorry about all that," Juanita said as she pushed herself up from the table. "You want your usual today?"

"Sure. Why not?" Ralph said with that little smile he always carried at the corners of his mouth.

Juanita was standing at the register with Jack, the manager, as Ralph Garman hobbled out the door after lunch, leaning heavier on his cane than usual.

"Did you hear about Glenn Farley, Mr. Garman's friend?" she asked.

"Sure did," Jack said with a knowing nod.

"Got married at his age and moved to Kentucky. Can you believe it?"

"Got married?" Jack said, looking sharply at her. "He died last week. Didn't you see it in the paper?"

# CARDS

Five of them played poker the third Friday night of every month. They had been doing this for the past eleven years. The original gang was still intact after all this time and usually the only occasions that called for a substitute were vacations, sickness or the very rare family commitment (such as a graduation or wedding) that just couldn't be moved. Most of them had had to miss a couple of times through the years. Harry went to the beach with his wife and kids every June; George had a series of surgeries a few years back; Randall missed twice for his wife's family reunions until he finally just put his foot down and refused to ever go to one again. Eddie broke his arm at work in what he called "the fall of '09" and laid out for two consecutive games because he couldn't shuffle or deal and Toby, bless his stout and stubborn heart, was the only one who could boast of never missing a game or a sandwich. None of these times was ever a threat to cancelling a poker game. One of the remaining four always had a friend or someone they worked with who would step up and fill the vacant chair. Such was the case that Friday night in April when confirming the next month's game.

"By the way, fellows, I can't be here next month," Toby announced as they all were counting their losses and wins and getting ready to call it a night.

"What!" the other four yelled as close to unison as you can get without a rehearsal.

"I know. I know. I've never missed a game. But next month is our 25th anniversary and, well, you know. It's kinda hard to say no."

"I'm ashamed of you, Toby old boy," Randall chimed in without looking up from his stacks of chips. "You give in on this

42

# HALF & HALF

one and you will have to celebrate the 50th one, too. Don't do it, boy."

They all laughed until Harry brought up the dreaded substitute. "If you're the one gone, then you have to get the fill-in. Who's it going to be? You got somebody in mind or you want one of us to get somebody?"

"I got a cousin who has been wanting to play for years," Toby said. "Boris Platino. Any of you know him?"

"Boris? Who is named Boris?" Eddie asked as he pushed his meager stack of white chips toward George, the host, to cash in.

"My cousin is named Boris, that's who. He's a weirdo but a pretty good poker player. You guys can stand him for one night and then I promise you I'll never, ever, miss another game."

"Famous last words," George mumbled as he counted out the ones, fives and tens to the winners and losers around the table.

The game started about 7:15 on a warm May evening. Introductions were made around the table and opinions began forming about their visiting player, Boris. After about an hour and a half, Randall admitted to himself the new guy was turning out to be as odd as his name, but he consoled himself that it would only be for one game. How bad could it be?

Harry, who was hosting this month, tried to overlook Boris' headband and pinky ring, but could not keep himself from thinking how nice it would have been of Toby to have sent someone a little more compatible to the crowd.

The biggest smile was on George's face because he was raking in most of the pots while Boris the Bore, sitting across the table from him, was cashing in for more chips after every other hand. He didn't care much for their guest's dirty fingernails or that thing on his head, but he sure liked his money.

Eddie was the first to push back from the table and say, "It's time for a beer and something to eat. What do you say, guys?"

43

# Don Reid

All the rest chimed in their agreement and made a move toward the kitchen. All except Boris, who kept his seat while rubbing his eyes with the palms of his hands.

"Want something to eat?" Eddie asked, mostly out of duty.

"Naw. I need to just sit here a minute alone and find my center. I need to core, you know what I mean?" Boris asked, still rubbing his face.

"You need to *core*?" Eddie asked a little confused. "You know where the bathroom is, don't you, pal?"

"Naw, man. Core. Focus. These cards are setting me on fire. Don't you feel it?"

Eddie looked out to the kitchen where all the others had gathered and wished they were hearing what he was hearing because he wasn't sure how to respond.

Boris continued with his soliloquy, his eyes still tightly clenched. "I get five cards and they say one thing to me and then I have to throw, say, two or three away, and then those five are saying something different. I get all the messages and they confuse me. They scare me. I do not know and cannot know which is the real message. It's taking the breath out of me."

Eddie looked through the kitchen door from the den where they were playing and motioned for Randall to come join them.

"What's the message, pal?" Eddie asked condescendingly.

Boris looked slowly up at him and while rubbing his beard with both hands, asked, "Do you not know what each card says?"

"What it says?" Eddie asked, looking sideways more at Randall than at Boris who was still seated at the table.

"Yes, says. Each card has a meaning. A life meaning. You can tell a man's fortune with this deck of 52 cards. Tarot? Nonsense. These are all the cards you need. You want your fortune told, friend?"

"Not necessarily," Eddie said quickly.

"Sure," Randall answered, taking another bite of his sandwich.

44

# HALF & HALF

Boris picked up the deck, shuffled it and handed it to Randall and said, "Deal three cards from anywhere in the deck. Just lay them on the table facedown."

Randall set his drink and salami sandwich down and did as he was instructed. Boris reached for the first card and turned it over. It was the two of hearts.

Boris looked straight ahead as he spoke, "Deuce of hearts. There will be a change in your love life." Then he turned the second card.

"Seven of spades is the card of betrayal. Do you want to see the third card?"

Randall hesitated for just a second. It surprised him that his breathing was catching. "Sure," he said a little weaker than he intended.

"Three of spades. Are you sure you want to know what this card means?"

Boris' question was met with total silence in the room that had now filled with all the poker partners standing in a circle around the table. He waited for a few more beats, then without getting an answer of consent or denial, he said, "The black trey is the card of infidelity. But not yours. The infidelity of your wife. It's been going on for months; maybe longer. You can stop it, but you won't. You won't because you don't believe me. But you will and you will suffer. I wish I could help."

Randall didn't move. He stood staring at this stranger who had invaded their friendly game night and brought everyone down with this dark and personal prediction.

It was George who finally broke the silence to either save his friend, Randall, further embarrassment or to keep him from clocking this longhaired fool up beside the head. "Hey, Boris. Do me."

Boris shuffled and handed the deck to George while everyone watched in silence. He instructed him to, also, deal any

45

three cards on the table face down. Then, in the same manner as before, he turned them up, one at a time.

"Ten of clubs. Stress. A card showing great stress. King of hearts. You may want me to stop."

"No, I don't want you to stop. What does the King of hearts mean?" George was adamant.

"It means your health is affected. A card of certain bad health. Are you sick?"

"No."

"Well, you will be soon. Count on it. And the third and last card…five of diamonds. It means, and I'm sorry to have to say this but you said you wanted the truth. It means a passing is imminent."

For the first time Boris looked up from the table and directly into George's eyes. He spoke firmly but with a sadness in his voice, "You'll be dead in three months."

"Get out. Get the hell out of my house." Harry spat the words out as he pulled the man out of his chair by the back of his shirt. No one in the room made a move to stop him or to offer any help to Boris. "Move," was all Harry said as Boris left the house through the kitchen while putting his jacket on. None of the players moved until they heard the backdoor opening and shutting.

After an awkward period of at least a dead minute, Eddie said, "Whose deal is it?"

"I'm not in the mood anymore. Let's call it a night," Randall said, sounding suddenly tired.

No one disagreed or even said a word of agreement. They just all sat down and counted the chips at their places at the table and pushed them to the host, Harry, to be cashed in. Except when Harry went to get the dish in the kitchen where they always placed their money when buying chips, it was empty.

# FLAG

Ricky had been looking forward to the sixth grade ever since he set his foot in his first grade classroom. Sixth grade was the year he could try out for the middle school baseball team. Sixth grade was when he would have more than one teacher; he would get to go to other rooms for Math, Science and English. And sixth grade was when he could volunteer to raise the flag every morning before classes, then lower and fold it every afternoon at the close of the school day. He could remember sitting in his first grade class, Miss Carrier's room, and watching out the window as Buddy Coiner, his next door neighbor and Charlie Easton, his best friend's older brother, would march out and back to the flag pole and do their American duty with pride and dedication. He knew from that first day of school that he wanted to be one of those boys.

He and Freddie Easton had talked about it a thousand times. In the second grade they watched twice a day out the window; in the third grade, they even got scolded for not paying attention as their eyes followed the Stars and Stripes up and down that pole with each pull of the rope. In the fourth and fifth grades, he and Freddie were each in rooms that were robbed of a view of the activities around the flagpole in the a.m. and p.m. of each day. But that never deterred their dream or dampened their enthusiasm. They still wanted to be those two boys. The two boys who carried, raised and lowered the national banner no matter the season. They would gladly put on their heaviest coats, earmuffs, gloves, stocking caps and brave twenty-degree weather, looking into twenty mile per hour winds, just to pull the rope. They had it all worked out. Ricky would pull in the mornings and Freddie would pull in the afternoons. Ricky would carry the flag out and Freddie would carry it in. It was all settled.

# Don Reid

Only one more thing to do to finalize their five-year plan. How do you get to be the flag boys?

"Mrs. Hinson," Ricky said in a hushed voice as he stood beside his fifth grade teacher's desk. "Do you know how you get to be one of those boys who take the flag up and down? Freddie and I want to do it next year."

"I can honestly say I don't know anything about that, Ricky. I suggest you stop at the office and ask Mr. Moody. And you should do that pretty soon. There's only three more days of school, so don't put it off."

"Can Freddie and I go to the office now and ask him?"

She looked at the clock at the back of her room. Why not? The day was nearly over and summer vacation was already seeping into the fabric of their schedules. Very little schoolwork would get done any more this week. Mentally, school was over, and no one was happier about this than Mrs. Hinson.

Ricky and Freddie stood in the principal's outer office and asked the school secretary if they could see him. Mr. Moody heard them and came to the doorway smiling.

"What's up, boys?"

Because Freddie never did, Ricky spoke for both of them. "Mr. Moody, how do you get to be flag boys?"

"Well, I usually just let whoever asks. If nobody asks, I just appoint two."

"Can we do it next year?" Ricky almost yelled.

Mr. Moody took out his pen and walked to the counter than ran across the front of the outer office. "I'll write your names down right now. Freddie Easton and Ricky Sandridge. There you go. It's done. You boys be here about ten minutes before school starts the first day in September and I'll walk you through it the first couple of times. You won't have any trouble."

"Thank you so much," Ricky said over his shoulder as he went out of the office in an end-of-school glee.

## HALF & HALF

Freddie even managed to quietly say, "Thank you, Mr. Moody."

And their dream had come true. Come September, they would be the boys the first, second and third graders watched out the windows each day. They would be the strutters carrying the colors in and out of the school office and picking it up from and placing it on the shelf beside the secretary's desk. It was enough for them to wish that the next school year was starting tomorrow.

As the summer swiftly blew by and the days of baseball and swimming started to show tiredness by growing longer and slower, it was the one thing that kept a spark in Ricky's eye. As much as he dreaded school, he couldn't wait to be one-half of the flag boy team.

And then the phone rang.

"Hello."

"Ricky? This is Freddie."

"Okay, I know who it is, you idiot."

"I've got some bad news. My dad is getting transferred and we're moving."

"What? When? Where?"

"North Carolina. And right away. We've already put a for sale sign in our front yard. I'll start to school down there next week."

"What about the flag?"

"What?"

Ricky immediately regretted he had said that. He should have said he was sorry Freddie was going and how much he would miss him. But all he could think about was the flag boys. Who would be the other boy? They had planned on this for five years and now, just five days before they are ready to make their first carry, no Freddie. Sure, he was sorry Freddie had to move. How could Freddie's dad do this to them? How could he spoil their dream and rip their plans in shreds? Why couldn't he get

49

Don Reid

another job here and stay home and let Freddie do what he had wanted to do since the first grade? Boy, life could really be crappy, couldn't it?

Ricky's mother had made the call for him to the school principal. Mr. Moody laughed and told her he would salve Ricky's disappointment a little by letting him pick his own new flag partner. He told her he would email a list of all the students that would be in Ricky's sixth grade class and then he could call whomever he wished to team up with for the two daily trips to the flagpole. All he had to do was contact them and get their consent.

Three days before the start of school and Ricky Sandridge's world was in a spin. He studied the names of all the boys in his class and found himself not caring to spend that much time with any of them. But he had to make a choice. He ran his finger down the list of the 23 students again but this time he stopped on a name he had yet to consider. Wow! Why hadn't he thought of this before? This was risky and it could be embarrassing. What if he got a no instead of a resounding yes? But then… what if he got a yes? It was well worth the risk he decided as he went to the phone book, looked up the number and dialed.

"Hello."

"Hello, is this Mary Jane Taylor, the prettiest girl in school?"

"Is this Ricky?"

"Yes, it is and I've got something to ask you that might really be fun."

Ricky Sandridge was growing up.

50

# GREEN

It was 1954 and Paul Tanner was fresh out of journalism school. His first job was in the small, one-paper town of Corbin, Virginia. Twenty-two years old, alone and scared, he found himself working for an ego with a bowtie who thought of himself as a modern day Horace Greely. Lester Potter, pronounced 'Les is Potted' behind his back by everyone on the staff, considered his years as editor-in-chief as his ticket to demean and embarrass everyone in his employee. Especially the young, the alone and the scared.

"Tanner, here's your first assignment. Get it quick and get it right. You know anything about football?"

"Enough," Paul Tanner answered back while looking at the sheet he had been handed.

"Well, it's Friday night. That spells high school football in every town, large or small, in America. And the smaller the town, the bigger deal it is. Be there at kickoff and get the color and make it sound better than it was. This should be an easy one if you learned anything at all in that dinky little college you graduated from."

"That dinky little college from which I graduated," Paul corrected with a smile. But as soon as the words had flown out of his lips, he knew how badly he had erred. His boss glared silently at him without a smile until Paul backed out of the office, that smelled strongly of cigar smoke and whiskey, and disappeared from the doorway.

The game on the field behind Corbin High was, sure enough, like a thousand games being played all over the country that night. He watched the plays, described a few, printed the final score and turned the story in an hour before the 11:45 deadline. The next morning he found a note on his desk demanding he report to 'Les is Potted's' office immediately upon

51

his arrival. He wasted no time in striding up the stairs, three steps at a time, to get his well-deserved praise for a job well done.

"Tanner, that is the worst piece of garbage I have ever had to print in any paper I have ever been associated with."

"(With which I have been associated)" Paul wanted to say but didn't.

"You told the score. You spelled out the plays. But you hardly mentioned who made the points. This is a small town, Tanner. People want to see their names in the paper. They want to see their kids' names in the paper. Names sell papers. Don't you understand that simple rule of human nature? Are you just too green to know anything? Remember this rule in writing newspaper copy. Three things. Facts. Facts. Facts. You can never have too many facts. Now get out of here."

Three days later Paul got his next important assignment. He was informed, by a memo from Potter's office, to cover the Monday night meeting of the town council. So with pad and pencil in hand, he took a seat on the front row and followed the long and boring discussions about city pipelines and assessed taxes and the rezoning of residential boundaries. He wrote his story at his desk and again was well ahead of the nightly deadline for the morning paper.

And again, a note demanding an immediate appearance in the boss's office was lying on his desk when he arrived early the next morning.

"Tanner. How did you ever get out of that city college you went to?"

"(City college to which I went. And it wasn't a city college. It was a good four-year college that I am proud to have attended.)" Of course, all of this was said in Paul Tanner's head and not to Lester Potter's face. And yes, there is the offending

# HALF & HALF

cigar butt in the ashtray and the bottle on the side table is definitely bourbon.

"Every vote that came up last night in that meeting, you reported. Right here in black and white – 4 to 3 for; 4 to 3 against; and 3 to 3 with one abstaining. You told *how* they voted but you didn't tell *who* voted. Names, Tanner. I need names. The people need names. They want to know if Curry or Atkins or Skinner voted for or against the pipeline. If Houseman or Conners or Meeks voted for the rezoning. Don't you see how it matters? Facts. Facts. Facts. You can never have too many facts. Facts and names. Names and facts. That is what makes a newspaper story. You did learn the Who, What, When, Where and How didn't you, Tanner? Well, take note that Who is always first. Names, Tanner, and facts. Get out of here and go work the police files till you learn something. Till that green wears off and you learn how not to write like an amateur."

For Paul Tanner to deny his embarrassment and discouragement would have been a lie too heavy to carry. He considered just walking away from the job and applying for another one in another small town to get his feet wet and learn his trade. But it was while working through the menial police files, that had to be sifted through each night before deadline, that his next assignment became apparent. The police radio barked to the near empty pressroom that a bad wreck had just happened on state route 24. Three cars were involved and he could already hear the sirens as he rushed out the door and jumped into his vehicle and sped through the quiet downtown streets.

He was on the scene just behind the first arriving police officers. He kept his distance while at the same time staying close enough to see the wreckage firsthand. He saw the people from two of the cars standing on their own and moving about. It seemed only one person, the driver of the blue Chevrolet station

53

# Don Reid

wagon, was still in his car. And he wasn't moving. He sat slumped in the driver's seat while members of the rescue squad pried the left front door open and two of the attendants lifted the man out and lay him on a stretcher.

Paul's heart nearly stopped beating and his recent dinner began bubbling in his stomach. He knew that face. He knew that driver.

"Is he dead?" he asked the policeman standing near him with a flare in his hand.

"Dead drunk. You know who it is, don't you?" the cop, Sgt. Andy Miller, answered without taking his eyes off the action in front of him.

"I'm not sure. Who is it?"

"Your boss, 'Les is Potted'. And this ain't the first time. You writing up this story?"

"Yeah, I guess so," Paul said without much enthusiasm. "Is he going to be alright?"

"He'll be alright," Sgt. Miller said. "The drunks always live. But that ain't your problem is it, son? Your problem is you're here to write a news story." And then he chuckled a dry little laugh that wasn't really a laugh at all. "Just be sure you do what's right. Names and facts. That's what matters ain't it, son?"

# RAN

Arthur was not aware of every minute in his wakening hours anymore. He dozed a lot. He sat in his over-stuffed chair in his den where the afternoon sun streamed in and kept him warm on particularly bright days and his mind drifted easily from the moment to sometimes fifty or sixty years ago. And to tell the truth, if someone had asked, he rather enjoyed it. So many memories. So many years under his belt. So much to look back on and so little to look forward to. He could sit here and reminiscence selectively as he wished. He could squash the bad ones and savor the good ones and no one knew the difference but him. That was the true secret of growing old. Not caring anymore what other people thought. And he felt, on good days, he pretty much had that task mastered.

His biggest bother, of late, was never having a moment alone. It seemed someone in his family was there in the house all the time. Janie, his older daughter, slept over most nights now. Lizzie, his youngest, came after breakfast and spent most days cleaning and cooking for him. And Roger, his only son, was always there in the evenings after work taking care of whatever the house needed to stay in shape and often just sitting with him and watching television. They all appeared busy but Arthur knew in his heart why they were there. They were all keeping a watch on him because he could no longer be left by himself. He could still bathe and dress himself but it was no secret that he fell more and more all the time. The last two times he had seriously hurt himself though no bones had broken. But the large bruise on his forehead was proof enough he needed a family member around most every minute now. This afternoon it was his granddaughter, Tacy. She was on the sofa reading a book but he noticed she glanced his way every time she turned a page.

"What are you reading, girl? Something for school?"

"Yeah. *Wuthering Heights.*"

"I would have figured you had read that in high school."

"Well, to be honest, I did. But I really don't remember much about it and it was on our list for this year, so I thought I'd better read it again."

"I hated that book," Arthur said as he pulled the afghan from the back of his chair around his shoulders.

"I don't hate it," Tacy said, sitting up, "but I have discovered that I didn't understand much of it when I was in high school. It's more of a college read for sure."

"What year *are* you in college?"

"I'm a junior this year, Poppa. Next year, graduation. And you're coming and sitting on the front row."

"Don't count on it, sweetheart."

"But I am counting on it. No excuses. You'll be there."

Silence filled the next minute or two while the real cloud of their conversation settled into the room.

"Poppa, what do you miss most?"

Without pause, Arthur answered, "Your grandmother."

"That's *who* you miss most. I said *what* do you miss most?"

"Freedom. The freedom of going where I want to go and when I want to go. Not having to call your mother or your aunt or uncle to take me here and there. Just get in the car and go without answering to anyone or asking anyone. God knows, I hate asking. I hate that more than anything if 'what do you hate most?' is your next question."

Tacy laughed loudly at this along with Arthur and he was glad. He loved this girl, this young woman, and he always loved making her laugh.

"One more question, Poppa, and then I'll let you get back to your nap."

"Please," Arthur said, still smiling. "I don't want to do anything to get off schedule with my naps. Because then that

# HALF & HALF

would run into my next meal and then that would make me late for my next nap. I'm a busy, busy man, Tacy. Now what's the one more question?"

"Do you have any regrets?"

"Sure. Many."

"What do you regret most? The one that really bothers you when you think long on it?"

Arthur did think long on it. So long that Tacy thought he might have dozed off again. She had picked her book up and resumed reading when his voice startled her as it broke the heavy silence of the room.

"I was younger than you are now. About 19. Pretty loose and wild. And I knew this girl who had just gotten engaged. I asked her out and she wanted to go but she was scared her boyfriend would find out. But not too scared. She called me one night around midnight. I had my first apartment and a pretty good job for the times. She wanted to come over. I hope you're old enough to be hearing this story, girl."

"I'm 21, Poppa, and I have my own apartment, too. Go on with your story."

"Well, she came over and spent the night. Are you blushing, yet?"

"Not yet," Tacy said with wide eyes. And they laughed together again.

"But the girl had morals. She wouldn't even kiss me with her engagement ring on. So she took it off and put it in an ashtray by my bed. I didn't know this until the next morning after she left. She called me from work in a panic and said she had just missed it and asked if I would bring it by the department store where she was a clerk. She said I had to hurry because her boyfriend was taking her to lunch and she had to have it on when he got there. So downtown I went and turned the corner to go into the store with the ring in my hand and there stood Herman Gleason, waiting for me at the front door. 'Gimme 'at

57

ring,' he said. And when I put it in his hand, he sucker punched me just as hard as he could with the other hand, right in the face. I didn't go down, but my knees almost buckled. I kind of shook my head and then just stood there and looked at him. And for the life of me I could not bring myself to hit him back. I wasn't scared but I was shamed. I felt so bad about what I had done to him that I just couldn't bring myself to defend myself. So I ran."

"You ran?"

"No. I just turned around and slowly walked off without doing anything. So it was the same thing as running. Herman saw it that way, I'm sure. And I always hated that I didn't tell him why I didn't hit him back."

"But Poppa, you didn't run. You did the right and manly thing."

"Well, you may think so, but most men would see it the same as running. Not hitting back is running or at least that's the way a young man looks at things."

"But young men are sometimes fools who grow up to be wise and honorable men. I'll bet even Herman thinks so today."

"Ole Herman. He died in Viet Nam."

"And the girl?"

"I don't know. I just remember reading in the paper about Herman. And oddly, that is the regret I think of most. But I'm not sure if I regret the fact that I 'ran' or if I regret not telling Herman *why* I 'ran.' He never knew how bad I felt about what I had done to him."

"Poppa, I don't think you have anything to regret either way. You did something wrong with that girl and you felt so badly about it that you wanted to punish yourself. That's really why you didn't hit ole Herman back. I think you have carried around a regret that is just not worth the worry. And I think he knew why you just stood there and looked at him. He knew it took a

## HALF & HALF

better man not to defend a wrong that it did to hit back. Don't you think?"

Arthur never answered. When Tacy walked over to pull his blanket up, his head was to the side and his eyes were closed. She smiled to herself. He'll wake up in time for dinner. Poppa always does.

# RACE

Marci and Lisa stood in the middle of the restaurant and hugged. They had not seen one another in seven years. Facebook, emailing, texting and an occasional phone call kept them up to date on each other, but even all those techy experiences couldn't match an actual eye-to-eye hug. They lived in different states now but had known and loved each other since being born next-door-neighbors. Only two weeks difference in their ages and even a professional beauty pageant judge would be hard-pressed to say which was the prettier. Their whole lives had been one long and friendly race, a fact that did not go unnoticed by them. Even now they were aware of it.

"Who's going to let go first?" Marci asked through tears, still clinging to Lisa.

"Not me, girl. I'll stand here as long as you do," Lisa said, feeling her makeup running down her cheeks.

"Let's do it like we used to then," Marci suggested.

"Do you mean like on the count of three?"

"Like one, two, three and let go on four, or let go on three? I never could figure which one it was supposed to be."

This caused them both to shriek with laughter as they dropped their arms and sat down with all the surrounding tables of diners smiling at them.

"Everything was always a competition with us, wasn't it?" Marci stated more than asked.

"Oh, heavens. Who could finish their candy bar first. Who could jump rope longest without tripping," Lisa added.

"Who would kiss a boy first and go on a date first."

"My parents saw to it that you won that one," Lisa said. "They were stricter on me than Pam and Tony were on you. Are they doing okay?"

"They're fine. Getting older but who isn't?"

# HALF & HALF

Lisa's smile faded quicker than she meant it to. "You know, honey, we've carried that same competition right into adulthood, haven't we?"

"Oh, I don't know," Marci said thoughtfully. "Do you think we have?"

"Certainly I think we have. Now, tell me the truth. Didn't you feel a little pressure when I got married first? Be honest."

"Yeah, I guess a little. I was happy for you but I was a little jealous I suppose."

"Of course you were. And you want to know an even deeper truth about this race we have had all our lives? I was upset when your David was born. I just kept thinking you had beaten me to something we both wanted."

Marci looked stunned and then slightly amused. "Girlfriend, you didn't have to confess that one."

"I know I didn't but I feel closer to you than anyone in my life and I'm not ashamed to tell you that. Of course, I feel better about it now that I have three kids and you only have two."

And together they howled again like the old friends they were.

"You know what, honey?" Lisa said. "I think we were happiest when we did things at the same time. We graduated high school the same night. College the same month. They were the really fun times; when we didn't have any race for a prize we could hold over one another's head. Don't you think?"

"I think you're right," Marci agreed. "And then there is that one race that I'm glad you won."

"Heavens, which one was that?" Lisa asked, sipping her iced tea.

"The husband race. You've had two to my one, so I gladly give you the prize."

"Do you really? Gladly?"

"What?" Marci asked, truly puzzled.

61

"I mean are you so happy that you never think there might be someone else out there for you?"

"Yes. And I resent that just a little bit," Marci said with a drawn face.

"Oh, excuse me. Did we finally hit a subject, after all these years, too sensitive to share?" Lisa said, making her eyes big.

Marci leaned back in her chair and looked at her friend for a long time. Maybe thirty seconds. And that's a long time to stare into someone's eyes without a word spoken. Then finally she found the right words to say. "I'm in love with Richard as much as I was the day I married him."

"No you're not," Lisa said as she picked up a dinner roll and began buttering it. "Tell it to the Boy Scouts. This is me you're talking to, Marci. Me. Remember? No secrets between us. Always the truth. But that's okay. If you think you're happy, that's just as good as being happy."

"You're more of a cynic than you used to be, Lisa," Marci said with no malice in her voice.

"Oh, you have no idea, my dear old friend. Tell me this: would you rather be rich or happy?"

"Happy," Marci said without hesitation.

"That's because you're rich. Let's try another one. Would you rather be healthy or happy?"

"That's unfair."

"You have to pick one."

"Okay then, happy."

"Then maybe you've won," Lisa conceded with her palms pointing upward.

"Won what?" Marci asked, a little irritated.

"The Race. The Race we have been running all our lives. Who could hold their breath the longest. Who could eat the most ice cream. Who could kiss the most boys our senior year. Remember? Whatever the competition has been for, you have taken the prize and you're welcome to it."

# HALF & HALF

"Wait a minute," Marci said. "Happiness is the prize? Is that what this has been about all our lives? All this winning was to bring us happiness?"

"I think so," Lisa said with a nod. "And if you think you're happy, then you are. If you have moments of doubts, you can tell yourself it's just a passing mood. But if you smile more than you cry, you're happy."

"Do you smile more than you cry?"

"On the good days I do," Lisa said, almost to herself as she stared down at her hands.

"Has this conversation made a wrong turn someplace?" Marci said, trying to lighten things a bit.

"Maybe so. Let's talk about something else," Lisa said, looking for a waiter.

"Or some*body* else. That's always fun," Marci laughed.

"Yeah, let's talk about Angie Baker or Laura Hammond. That always cheered me up. But let's order first. And, oh yeah, Connie Taylor," Lisa said in a whisper. "You're not going to believe who she's having an affair with." Then louder, "Waiter, I think we're ready to order."

# SURPRISE

It was a beautiful June evening. The sun was still hot as they began to arrive and gather on the parking lot behind the gym. Roger stood and talked nervously with his other classmates until Mrs. Trotter came to the door of the cafeteria and waved for all of them to come inside. With caps and gowns in hand, they slowly headed for the door, all laughing a little too loudly and hugging one another a little too much. Everyone vied for a place in front of a couple of temporary full-length mirrors to get a last look at themselves in their respective black or white gowns and caps with the tassels hanging in their eyes.

Mr. Hanniford, the assistant principal (remember the difference between principle and principal is the head of your school is always spelled with p-a-l at the end because he is your PAL- third grade spelling lesson), stood on a chair, raised his hands and shouted for everyone to be quiet. He made an attempt at a corny speech about being the last time he could tell all those present what to do and about half laughed and the other half sneered. Then he went on to say, "Now students, I want you all to straighten up your mortarboards and please do not wear them on the side of your head. Center them on the crown of your noggin and then reach up and place your liripipe, yes, class, that would be your tassel, on the right side. No, on your right. I see there are still some of you who don't know your right from your left. Once you have received your diplomas, I will instruct you, after you have returned to your seats, to stand and move your liripipes or tassels, if you prefer, to the left side simultaneously. What? That means all at once. Now please get in line the way we rehearsed yesterday."

As the class was milling about and finding their designated places in alphabetical order, Willy rushed up to Roger, grabbed him by the sleeve and nearly toppled him over as he pulled him toward a secluded corner of the room.

"Have you seen her yet?" he whispered almost inaudibly in Roger's ear.

"Seen who?" he asked, a little irritated.

"Maxine," Willy almost shouted.

"Maxine Hodge?"

"Yes," he said with a smile so big it was eating his entire face. "Everybody's talking about it and it's true."

"What's true?" Roger asked, a little more interested now.

"She ain't wearing anything under her graduation gown!" And this time Willy could hardly breathe out the words.

"Naw. You got to be kidding," Roger said a little skeptically. Slightly skeptical because Maxine Hodge had been known to do some rather unusual and unexpected things. Like the morning she was giving the announcements over the school intercom and was to announce that the school principal, Mr. Michael Randolph, would be in his office from 10 till noon for any student who needed to meet with him. She was dared to say, "Slick Mick Randy will be in his office...." And did. Slick Mick Randy didn't like it much but Maxine didn't seem to care. Or the time she was dared to put her lunch tray and utensils in the trash bin instead of separating them as she exited the lunchroom. She enjoyed the notoriety of this incident so much she continued to dump it all in the trash every day. There were many more incidents because no dare went unchallenged with Maxine. So maybe Willy was right – maybe Maxine *was* naked underneath her clothes.

After getting lined up in their proper order, Roger turned around and saw that Maxine was just two couples behind him. He caught her attention for just a second and she smiled at him and dropped her eyes. Roger followed her gaze to the hem of her gown as she raised it above her knees. He was convinced. Maxine was in full bloom at graduation and there was no doubt about it. Roger tried to find Willy to give him the nod, but the music started before he could spot him toward the back of the line.

There is something sobering about that melody. It's a cross between a funeral lament and a movie theme. It's inspiring, stirring and upsetting. From the time it began, it took hold of the entire senior class and melted them into a cadre of chills and tears. They marched down the aisle, for the very last time, past their parents and friends and took their seats. They sat restlessly and listened to the mayor of the city give the old Ambition, Dedication, Perseverance speech. Some minds wandered; some daydreamed; some dozed; and at one point Maxine, sitting four seats down from Roger, leaned forward, smiled at him and pulled her gown up past her bare knee to mid-thigh. As soon as he returned her smile, she leaned back in her seat as if to say, "Here it comes."

The name calling began. It started with Lenore Adkins and quickly, much too quickly, moved through the alphabet to the H's. Maxine was standing on the top step ready to proceed to the stage. She turned and looked at the students behind her and one last time at Roger as she winked and nodded her head. He knew it was coming but he just didn't know *what* was coming. Would she really flash the entire student body and all their families right here on graduation night? Wow! What a story and what a memory that will make, Roger kept thinking. Someone must have dared her and old Maxine never turned her back on a dare. Slick Mick Randy, standing center stage, called her name and Roger watched intently as she strode across the stage. She reached for her diploma with her left hand and shook SMR's hand with her right just as they all had been instructed to do. And then it happened. She stopped dead still, turned her back completely on the audience, and faced the back of the stage. She reached up with her free hand and began unzipping her gown. When it was fully open, she dropped it slowly from her

# HALF & HALF

shoulders and there she was for all to see. A newly graduated Maxine Hodge in her Jackson High gym suit. T-shirt and shorts. She stuck the diploma in the waistband of her shorts, backed up to the right hand side of the stage and did six handstand flips to the other side. She landed with a perfect split with her hands in the air. The crowd erupted in applause and laughter. Even Slick Mick and all his teaching staff joined in.

They had their memory for the ages as every graduation class wishes for and Maxine had her dare. Life is more fun when you don't know what's coming, and with Maxine, you never did.

# HENS

Rural, post war, Georgia was not a pretty sight. The late 1940's economical boost had yet shown no signs of reaching outside of Atlanta, Augusta and Columbus. The countryside had seen little change since the Depression and the inhabitants had grown used to the lifestyle of living hardscrabble poor. Electricity and all its accompanying luxuries were strangers to most of the self-surviving folks of Bibb County. The turn-in-the-road village, known as Creek, was a gas station that sold more three-cent ice cream cups than it did gallons of gas and three churches that kept their doors open, surely, only by the grace of God.

Rev. Horace Tucker, fresh out of seminary, took his first charge at one of these churches that sat in sight of the other two. All he brought to the back roads of this starving state was a suitcase of books and a blue serge suit in his 1941 Plymouth coupe. His little house was furnished with discarded and donated fixtures from members of the congregation of the One God Presbyterian Church so the only pictures on the walls were of other people's kinfolk. It was Mason-Dixon hot the day he arrived in April of 1948 and it was still hot the Sunday after Labor Day. That was the afternoon he answered a knock at his front door.

"You the new preacher at One God?"

"I am that, sir," Horace answered firmly and formally.

"Well, I'm Bev Wingfield. I'm the preacher over there at the Non-Denominational Church of Jesus. I've been meaning to come say hello to you all summer but I farm and there just ain't no time, day or night, for visiting."

"I understand, Rev. Wingfield. Won't you come in?"

"Can't. No, I can't stay. I have to take my wife to see her sister up in Virginia in a couple of weeks. I've got help on the

68

## HALF & HALF

farm but I need you to help me on Sunday. If I move my service to 10 a.m., would you consider filling in for me before your eleven o'clock service?"

"Certainly I would. I'd be honored."

"Just preach the same sermon you preach at your church and that will be fine. As far as all this denominational stuff goes, I say it's all ice cream. We're just different flavors."

Not knowing exactly how to react to that last statement of faith, Horace decided not to and just smiled. In a few more short words of goodbye, he assured Bev Wingfield he would be there on the Sunday designated and wished him a good and safe trip north.

The inside of the sanctuary and even the faces of the congregants varied little from those of his own church. He sang their hymns with them, prayed with them and then preached to them, the same words of danger and comfort he would preach again that morning to his Presbyterians. Nary a word differed in his message – only in his praying. He did remember to change debts to trespasses in the Lord's Prayer. And when the service had ended and he had shaken every hand that stretched out to him, one grabbed him roughly by the sleeve as he was about to exit the front door.

"Preacher, I'm the head deacon here. My name's Smitty."

"Smitty. Nice to meet you."

"I have your pay for preaching. Where you want me to put it?"

"Put it?" Horace asked with sincerity and wonder.

"I'll just put it in your car if that's okay with you. That was a good sermon."

And Smitty was gone as quickly as he appeared.

Horace spoke to a few more folks who had gathered by the door and assured them he would be available to them or any of the congregation, all week long, who might need his services for any reason. Then he walked around to the side of the church

69

building to get into his car. That's when he saw Smitty stuffing something in the back seat.

"Smitty, what are you doing?"

"Just puttin' these chickens in the car. There was no room up front."

"Why are you putting chickens in my car?"

"They're your pay for preaching this morning. They're broiler hens. All three of them. Ready to eat, too. You can bring that coop back and just leave it on the church steps. I'll pick it up one day when I'm comin' by."

Horace wished many times hence, that he had said something. Even something clever or funny would have made for a good story. But he said nothing. He had another church service to do and then he would deal with Smitty's chickens.

After a Sunday lunch alone, of soup and a toasted cheese sandwich, Horace stood looking out the window to his backyard. There sat that smelly coop with the three hens still inside. Their fate was his decision and he had no idea what to do with them. Raised on the city streets of Louisville, he had never come in contact with a live chicken. He knew he couldn't keep them and certainly was not going to kill them. Maybe he would give them to a local farmer but only if he could keep it quiet. He would never want anyone from the Church of Jesus to learn that he was not appreciative of their generous gift. His thoughts were suddenly interrupted by someone approaching the chickens and looking in the coop. It was a boy, maybe ten or eleven years of age. Horace walked out the backdoor and spoke to him.

"Afternoon, young man."

"Hello. I'm just looking at your chickens. What are you gonna do with 'em?"

"I'm not real sure. Do you know anything about chickens?"

"Yeah. I know everything about 'em. These three are mine."

"Yours? How so?"

# HALF & HALF

"My daddy gave 'em to you this mornin'. They were kinda my pets and I'd sure hate to see you cut their heads off."

"What's your name?"

"Bobby."

"Bobby, I have no intention of cutting their heads off. You say they are your pets?"

"Yessir. I've even named 'em. I call 'em Ruth, Naomi, and Sarah. From the Bible, you know?"

"Yes, I know. Bobby, I don't want your pets. You can have them back."

"Really?" The boy beamed and wiped tears from both eyes. "Really, can I?"

With Horace's assurance Bobby thanked him profusely and climbed on his rusty old bike and headed down the lane with a promise to come back before dark and retrieve his three precious hens. And he must have, because when Horace Tucker looked out his back window as he washed dishes after supper, Ruth, Naomi and Sarah were gone, along with the coop.

It was nearly three weeks later that Horace ran into Smitty at the Ocmulgee Farmer's Co-op store just outside of Macon.

"Those broilers good?"

"Smitty. How are you, sir?"

"I'm fine. Those broilers good? And you never did bring my coop back."

"Smitty, I gave those chickens and your coop back to your son weeks ago."

Smitty stared at the young preacher longer than a pitcher has ever stared at a catcher waiting for the right signal. And when he spoke, Horace was more confused than ever.

"Preacher, I ain't got no son. Two girls. And I sure would like that coop back."

Horace stood silently watching Smitty climb into his battered old Ford pickup and pull away from the store. What

71

had happened here? But that was not the question. What had happened three weeks ago to his chickens? That was the question. And who was Bobby? That was an easy one. Bobby was a kid who had conned a young preacher from the city out of his Sunday pay. Maybe for need. Maybe for fun. He may never know. Those tears may have been real but more likely were crocodile. And as he shopped through the aisles for his weekly groceries, a Bible verse kept running through his head. Matthew 25:35. King James Version. *I was a stranger and ye took me in.*

Horace had to smile. Ruth, Naomi, and Sarah. And then he actually stood in the aisle and laughed out loud.

# ROAD

Jacob had been on the road for two hours and had already been lost three times. The farm he was in search of seemed to just fall off his GPS as soon as he crossed the first mountain. His directions showed he had two more small North Carolina mountains to cross but without the map that he used to keep in his car years ago, he had no certain idea of where he was going. Just ahead was the first gas/convenience store he had seen this morning. Surely someone there could get him back on the right road.

"I'm looking for the Berrycove Farm and Kennel," Jacob told the rotund man sitting on a stool behind the counter.

"You got a ways to go," was the only answer he received.

"Well, could you help me? It's on county Route 24 and I have taken a wrong turn someplace."

"You sure have, pal. Tell you what, go about four miles straight down the way you're going and turn left on 158. You'll go through, aw, a couple of little towns, just stops in the road really, and after about 25 miles you'll see a sign that says 30 miles to Berrycove."

"Thank you very much," Jacob said as he headed toward the door.

"And you can just turn your GPS off cause they tend to act up in these mountains," the voice behind the counter advised, followed by a nearly inaudible chuckle. The large man on the stool picked up his phone and began to dial as Jacob closed the door behind him.

It was a beautiful summer day and the tall trees and thick woods on each side of the road cast heavy shadows with bursts of sunshine intervals. From second to second he needed sunglasses and then didn't. The frequency of this pattern gave him a headache. That may have been why he didn't see it lying in the middle of the road until he was right on it. The brakes on his Volvo screamed as he slid nearly sideways to miss the crutch in his path. He pulled to the side of the road and that is when he saw, 50 feet in front of him, someone lying on the shoulder of the country road. He ran toward the body and saw it move just as he knelt by its side. It was a young woman, approximately 20 years old with another crutch lying beneath her. She was dressed in shorts and a t-shirt and the fact that she was pretty was obvious at just a glance.

"Are you alright?"

"I'm fine," she said, seeming more embarrassed than injured. "I slipped crossing the road and lost my balance. I am so sorry."

"It's okay. Here let me help you up. Where are you headed?"

"I was on my way to the grocery store for my grandmother just down the road here. I do this all the time and I have never fallen before."

"Well, let me get you in the car and I'll take you to the store."

Jacob got her back to his vehicle, belted her in and propped her crutches against the seat. As he got back under the wheel, she smiled appreciatively and said, "My name is Georgia. What's yours and what are you doing out here on this lonesome road?"

"I'm Jacob Conner. I'm out here looking for Berrycove Farm. There's a kennel there that raises Cavalier King Charles spaniels and I've got an appointment to buy one for my wife. It's our tenth wedding anniversary. It's a surprise."

"Oh, wow. That is really nice. Aren't you the perfect husband!"

"Don't know about perfect, but I try," Jacob said with a smile. "Where is this store you were headed toward."

"A little farther on. Just keep going."

"Did you hurt yourself when you fell?"

74

# HALF & HALF

"No. I'm fine. Do you see that little pull off area right there? Just pull in there for a minute," Georgia said with a little urgency in her voice.

As Jacob pulled off the road, the girl quickly popped the glove compartment open and pulled out a handful of papers that included his vehicle registration and stuffed them into her shorts.

"Hey! What are you doing?"

"Don't worry about it, big boy. Just give me a hundred dollars and I'm out of your car and out of your life."

"What?"

"I have your registration to prove I've been inside your car. I have your license number memorized – MJZ-407 – and if you don't want me calling the cops and telling them you picked me up and sexually assaulted me, then give me a hundred dollars and right now."

"Do you think I'm an idiot? Get out of my car."

"Think twice, Jacob. This ain't the first time I've done this and it can get real messy with that young wife of yours. She will wonder why you ever had me in the car and that crutch in the middle of the road is a pretty tall tale to swallow. One hundred bucks is a small price to pay. I'm getting out but I won't go away if you pull off. I'll call the sheriff and they will pick you up before you cross the next mountain."

Georgia threw her crutches out the window and then flung the door open and hopped out on both feet with no signs of an injury in either of her limbs. She slammed the door, then stood by the car and sneered as she said, "Hundred bucks, Jacob. Small price to pay."

"Give me back the registration first."

"When you hand me the money."

Jacob thought about it but not for long. He reached in his front pocket and took out his money clip. He peeled off four 20s

# Don Reid

and two 10s and handed them out the passenger window to the girl standing in the weeds.

"Give me the registration," he demanded.

"In your dreams, cowboy. Move it and just hope I don't decide to use any of these papers I've still got stuffed in my pants. They're my insurance."

Jacob thought about taking them away from her, but knowing what he would have to do to get them, he decided against it and simply put the transmission in drive and pulled off, leaving her standing along the road waiting for her next victim.

It was nearly twenty miles before he even met a car or saw signs of any life such as a house and certainly not a service station. Georgia had a game that was stacked against him. And the more he thought about it, the more he was sure there was nothing he could do at this point. He would just have to suck it up, pick up his dog and try to find another road home.

# BUNGLE

Benny Staples hated the nickname "Benny the Bungler" as anyone would. But that was how he was known throughout his hometown and for good reason.

At 21 years of age, Benny had no record with the law in Bedford, Virginia until he walked into the local branch of the F&M bank with an empty paper sack and a Bill Clinton Halloween mask on and demanded the sack be filled with money and on the double. His command was met and he rushed out of the two-teller, Holly Street bank office and sprinted to his waiting 1994 Dodge Spirit. He tossed the money in the back seat and reached for the keys in his pocket as he slipped into the driver's seat. That's when the unexpected happened. The car keys flew out of his sweaty hand and fell between the seats. He scrambled to reach them with the tips of his fingers and even fumbled in the glove compartment for a stick or a ruler or something that would be thin enough to scoot the keyring out to where he could grab it. But all this was to no avail. While Benny was still trying to retrieve his keys, the police arrived and gave him much more to worry about.

In the long run, they gave him only five months to serve in the county jailhouse. All other time was suspended because this was his first- ever offense. And also because all of the $1,200 was recovered as Benny had no time to spend any of his ill-gotten fortune from the time he left the front door of the bank until he reached his car parked twenty feet away.

Benny's size, five feet six, and his mass of red curly hair made him an easy target in and out of confinement. Everyone joked with him and called him Benny the Bungler to his face. Their entertainment became his bane and he silently swore to make his name one they would remember but never again laugh at.

Having come to the conclusion that his vehicle was the sole reason for his capture, his next adventure, almost a year later to the day, was planned and executed afoot. It was a small branch just two blocks from his apartment. He walked there on Monday morning and was waiting when the front door was unlocked by one of the two lady tellers. Benny pushed his way inside and showed both women he had a gun.

"This is a .32 caliber pistol and I'll use it on you in a minute. Fill up this bag and none of that money with exploding ink on it. I know your tricks."

Both women stood staring at this small redheaded boy wearing a Richard Nixon mask and work gloves. Was he serious? Was this a joke? But he did have a gun so they obeyed his wishes and saw him tuck the bag under his arm and run toward the door. As luck would have it, Benny's luck anyway, an overweight lady in a wheelchair was pushing the front glass door open as he reached to pull it toward him. She saw the small pistol in his grip and threw both hands to her cheeks and screamed in horror. Her wheelchair remained frozen in the center of the doorway, obstructing Benny's route of escape.

"Get out of the way," Benny yelled and tried to free the chair from the door passage, but the fat lady just kept screaming. Benny grabbed the arms of the wheelchair and tugged with all his might to get her inside the bank. In doing so, he dropped the bag of money from under his arm and it got tangled in the large circular wheels. Now he had the lady and her chair inside but the moneybag was stuck under the chair. An alarm began to sound off behind him and the perspiration running down the back of his shirt (and also his pants) told him it was time to go.

Benny ran as hard and fast as he had ever run in his life and never stopped until he was inside his apartment with all the blinds pulled.

The police visited him within the hour, but they had no proof. The Richard Nixon mask was gone. There had been no

## HALF & HALF

fingerprints. Only the two tellers' description of a short, red haired man. Everyone knew, but no one had the proof, so the local law enforcement let it go but flagged Benny as someone to keep a close eye on.

Three months passed before someone of that height and attitude walked into the Altavista Loan Company with a full-headed Alf mask on and a .32 caliber pistol. (The mask was one Benny's older brother had worn on Halloween one year that he had recently found in his mother's attic.) Frank Dover was sitting at his desk when he looked up and aptly asked, "What the..."

"Just do what I say and nobody will get hurt. Put all your money in this bag or you'll be sorry you didn't."

"What money? We don't have any money here."

"What do you mean," Benny asked through the thick, hairy mask.

"This is a loan company. A branch office. All our money is on computer. We don't have fifty cents in this place."

At this point a large, six foot- four man of 60 years and 220 pounds came out of the back. He was dressed in a gray suit and tie and was obviously the manager.

"What's going on here?" he asked.

"Well, George, this thing here is trying to rob us," Frank said with a smile as Benny stood still in the center of the room, sweating profusely under his Alf mask.

"Rob us?" George repeated.

"I have a .32 caliber pistol here and I'm not..."

But before Benny could finish his statement of terror, George, who had seen his share of football fields and under matched fights, fluidly, yet precisely, kicked Benny in the groin with the toe of his well-polished, wing tipped Florsheim shoe. As Benny crumbled to the floor, writhing in pain, George reached down and took the .32 caliber pistol from his hand and the Alf mask from his head. As his red curls spread over his head, Frank and George looked at one another with surprise and amusement.

"Benny the Bungler," George laughed, putting the pistol in his suit coat pocket while Frank dialed the local police.

Benny's stay with the state was appreciatively longer this time. Of course, that only gave him more time to expertly plot his next escapade that would certainly lead to the fame and fortune he dreamed of with each passing day. "Just wait," Benny said to himself each night before falling asleep. "Just wait."

# DIFFICULT

He sat in his car in front of her apartment for a full fifteen minutes before opening the door and getting out. He ran every word of what he wanted to say at least three times over in his head. Each time he changed it a little bit and added to it and yet, none of the versions felt right. He wasn't sure if he should be sketchy with the facts or try to explain them in extreme detail. Should he ask her to be quiet while he talked or should he encourage her to interject her feelings and then play off her words and questions? Didn't matter. There was no good way to tell a woman you had been seriously seeing for three years and who thought an engagement ring was coming with every birthday or holiday, that you were breaking up with her. Women just don't seem to take it well no matter how you tell them. They are an emotional lot and never react the way a man does to such situations. He knew there would be tears; certainly hurt feelings; maybe even anger. But he could let that deter him no longer. When she opened the door and met him with that beautiful, innocent smile, he would just have to jump into it. Just do it. No pausing. No easing into it. Do it. And do it now.

"Hi, honey. How are you doing?"

"Judy, we have to talk and we might as well do it right now?"

"What?" she laughed. "Don't I even get a hello or a kiss? What in the world is so important that...?"

Todd had already pushed through the doorway and was standing in the middle of her living room before she even finished her sentence.

"Sit down. I need to say something."

Judy closed the door and sat slowly on the edge of her sofa without ever taking her eyes off him. She didn't speak and she also was no longer smiling. Her face held a hint of fear; a hint of bewilderment; and more than a hint of anger.

"Look, I have been sweating over how to say this so I'm just going to say it. I know we have been an item for nearly three years now. I know you think we should already be engaged and I know your parents think so, too. But the fact is, and this is the really hard part, the fact is I can't do this. I can't go on like this any longer. Tonight is it. We're breaking up and I'm sorry."

Judy's expression never changed. Her lips didn't part. Her brow didn't wrinkle. Her eyes never narrowed or lost their shine. She just stared at him in silence.

"Well, say something. Don't just sit there looking at me like that. Say something."

"Say something? I'll say something," she said with a little rise to her voice. "Why? What has happened?"

"That's just it," Todd said looking away from the sincerity in those glistening brown eyes. "I'm not sure. I'm just not cut out for this relationship. You have not done a thing. You are a good person. The sex is great. I like all your friends. I even like your family. And God knows I like you. I just don't… love you. Not in the way I know I need to for this to work for us."

Judy leaned her back against the pillows behind her on her sofa. "Who is it?"

"What do you mean, who is it?"

"Who are you seeing?"

"No, Judy it's not like that. I swear to you. I am not seeing anybody. I don't have anybody in mind. I promise you. It's just that I'm not in love with you. And I know that is a horrible thing to say and I can't tell you how difficult it is to speak those words to you. You have done nothing wrong and I am not seeing anyone. I just don't have the feelings I know I should have."

"You're a liar."

"No, I'm not."

"Yes, you are. What does she do for you that I don't do for you?"

# HALF & HALF

"She doesn't do anything for me."

"Then there is someone!"

"No, no. Listen to me. Do you have such a high opinion of yourself that you can't imagine that I just might not be in love with you? I mean that doesn't mean there's something wrong with you. It just means…I don't love you and I can't help it."

There was a long silence in Judy's second floor apartment while she slowly stood and walked down the hallway to her bedroom. She closed the door behind her while Todd simply stood in the middle of the living room floor and rubbed his hands through his hair. After what seemed like a half hour but was, in reality, more like ten minutes, he looked at his watch and wondered what she was doing in there. He walked to the bedroom door and said her name softly but to no avail. He tried the doorknob. It was locked. He called out to her again a little louder this time. And then he started to worry. What was going on in there? Was she just ignoring him or had she taken sleeping pills or cut her wrists? Every horrible scene he had ever read in a book or seen in a movie came back to haunt him and scare the living hell out of him.

"Judy! Answer me. Can you hear me? Open this door. Now or I'm coming through it. Do you hear me?"

The door flung open and Judy brushed past him dressed in her bathrobe and said, "Yeah, I can hear you. Shouldn't you be leaving now?"

"Not like this. I don't want to go with things like this."

"Oh, really? You want to stay until I say everything is okay? Until I say I don't blame you for not loving me anymore? Until I pat you on the back and say 'that's okay, Todd. I don't mind that you have turned my world inside out and left me sitting here in the dark, a trembling mess of nerves.' Is that what you want to hear before you leave?"

"Judy I don't think you realize how difficult this is for me."

83

"Difficult for you? Oh, boy. And you think it's a piece of cake for me? Just leave. And I hope you wreck and kill yourself on the way home."

"Thanks a lot. That's real classy."

"Don't talk classy to me, Todd Hinson. You are scum. Dirt under my feet. Just get out and I don't ever want to see you or hear from you again."

"Then you won't. You can count on it." And Todd slammed the door behind him and stormed down the steps to his car.

He sat with the motor idling for a few minutes before pulling out into the street. His stomach was churning just a little and his hands were shaking more than he wanted to admit as he sat there and thought to himself, 'Boy, that went from being the most difficult thing I ever did to the best thing I ever did. It was almost as bad as breaking up with Teresa. Except Teresa was a lot meaner and more dangerous than Judy. But at least this was a lot quicker than the time with Shirley. That one went on most of the night. Judy will be alright. She wasn't even crying when I left the way Susan had. Lord almighty, Susan sobbed and followed me all the way to the car. Every one of them is a little bit different. And, hey, I still have time to pick up Linda when she gets off from work. But, man, I will never, never let one go on for three years again. That is just too long. Too many feelings and promises all mixed up. Too many emotions. I don't know why they get so worked up. I swear, one of these days one of those crazy women is going to shoot me.'

# CHARITY

Dale Marvec had been chairman of the South Side Benevolent Fund for the past decade. His was a non-paying position but as he often joked, "it will look good in my obituary." The Fund had raised hundreds of thousands of dollars under his leadership and he could honestly say he was proud of the work all of those dollars had accomplished. Modest homes were built, medical bills had been paid, Christmas toys and clothes had been bought. So many had benefited from the hours he and his volunteer staff had put into the raising and spending of all those charity dollars.

Dale was in the process of closing the books on this fiscal year when he kept having trouble with the left column matching the right column. After three attempts, he walked out into Sharon Goodman's office and waited for her to get off the phone. Sharon had been the receptionist/secretary/bookkeeper even longer than Dale had been onboard and was the only paid employee on the staff. She knew all the ropes and how to pull them to make everyone happy. She motioned to Dale she would be off in just one short minute.

"Okay. Sorry about that, but that was Bud Master down at Master Tire Service and he was just promising to write a check for a thousand dollars. I didn't want to rush him."

"Absolutely not," Dave beamed. "But speaking of a thousand dollars, come in here and look at these books. I have a discrepancy of about nine thousand dollars I can't make heads or tails of."

Sharon followed him into his office and stood looking over his shoulder at the columns he was pointing out.

"This is showing, almost exactly, a shortage of a thousand smackers every month since March. Look here. For the year, it looks like $9300 has come in but I can't see where it was paid out or that we still have it on hand. See if you can make sense of any of this," Dale suggested as he pushed his chair back from the desk in order to give Sharon a closer vantage point.

She ran her finger down each column and turned the pages back month by month. With each turn, Dale noticed her hand shaking a little more uncontrollably. He looked up, for the first time, and saw how flushed her cheeks had become.

"Are you alright, Sharon?"

"Yes, I'm fine. Just..." She paused and swallowed hard and loud.

"Are you going to be sick?" Dale asked, now getting seriously alarmed.

"No, I'm okay. I just need to get a glass of water," she said as she rushed out of the room.

Dale sat at his desk, waiting for her to return. He absently leafed through the pages again and ran his finger from column to column on each month. Somewhere, in the midst of all this, the notion reluctantly sprang into his mind. But it couldn't be. Yet it made sense. But, Lord, it can't be. It has to be wrong. He walked to the outer office, stood by Sharon's desk and waited for her to come out of the restroom. When she did, her face was still red, her hands were still shaking and her eyes would not meet his. She walked determinedly to her desk and sat down heavily.

"Sharon, do we need to talk?"

"What do you mean?" she asked, not looking up from her fixed stare on the top of her desk.

"Do you know something about these losses that I don't?"

Now she looked up with growing defiance. "Are you accusing me of something, Dale?"

"I don't think I said anything close to an accusation. I just asked if you knew something about these losses."

"I don't like your tone."

86

# HALF & HALF

"I have no tone, Sharon. Look at me. I'm your friend. What's going on here?"

Somewhere about the "I'm your friend" line, the waterworks started and Sharon Goodman broke down and gave way to the tears. Dale Marvec waited patiently until her breath-grasping sobs subsided a little before he spoke again. He sat down in the chair in front of her desk and said, "Sharon, talk to me. I can see you have something that needs to be said. Talk to me."

"There's nothing to say. I needed the money and I took it. I always meant to put it back little by little, but I didn't. I just kept getting a little more each month. That's not who I am, but that's what I did."

"Do you have any of the money left?"

"Of course not. People don't steal to add to their savings account. They steal...well, for any number of reasons."

"And in the long run, Sharon, it really doesn't matter why one steals. I didn't ask you why because that doesn't matter. The fact that you did is what matters."

"Are you sure about that, Mr. Marvec? Are you sure it doesn't matter why?"

"What are you trying to say?" Dale asked, truly puzzled.

"I needed the money. That's what we do here, isn't it? We give money to people who need it. Well, I needed it so doesn't that make me the same as any other recipient?"

"You know better than that, Sharon."

"No, I don't. Need is need."

"But we offer it to them and you took it without anyone offering it to you. One is charity; the other is stealing. And you know that."

"I know no such thing. Do you even care what I spent the money on? Do you think I'm gambling or buying drugs? Well, I'm not. I'm using it on necessities. Bread and milk and rent and school clothes. The same reason we give to all those people who sign up at this very desk."

# Don Reid

"Why didn't you sign up like they do?"

"Oh, that is so easy for you to say. Do you know how embarrassing and demeaning it is to walk in here off the street and ask for money? For help? And then know that we are going to check out each individual story to see if there is any fraud involved. And then have to wait for a yes or no. I'm sorry, but I couldn't do it. I hate doing it to them and I couldn't do it to my family."

"Why didn't you come to me? I've never made you or anyone else feel ashamed to ask for help. Why didn't you talk to me?"

"I'm talking to you now, Dale. Let me, please, just take care of this with a little more time. Don't fire me. Don't turn me in. Let me pay it back. Try to think of me as one of those in need and give me another chance. I can't stand the embarrassment of anything more."

"I don't know if I can do that, Sharon. We have the Board, you know."

"The Board won't know if you don't tell them. I promise. And I'm begging you, please. We are a benevolent fund and I need your benevolence and your mercy. Please, for all the years we've worked together, give me a break."

ENDING NUMBER ONE: Dale Marvec gave Sharon Goodman a break. Two months later, the Board discovered the losses and charges were brought against them both. Sharon served two years for embezzlement and Dale Marvec was acquitted. However, he lost his job as VP of the consulting firm he had been with for fifteen years and he and his family left town and were never heard from again.

ENDING NUMBER TWO: Dale Marvec turned Sharon Goodman in and charges were brought against her. She served two years for embezzlement and, out of a revengeful heart, named Dale as an accomplice. Even though innocent, he was

# HALF & HALF

fired from his job of VP of a consulting firm due to the negative publicity and he and his family left town and were never heard from again.

ENDING NUMBER THREE: Dale Marvec showed total mercy and gave Sharon Goodman $9,300 out of his own bank account to cover her debt and never told anyone what had taken place. Two months later, his wife discovered the money missing from their personal account and traced the recipient to be Sharon Goodman. She filed for divorce and during the process her lawyers brought to the forefront the reason for the $9,300 payment. Charges were brought against Sharon and she served two years for embezzlement. Due to a morals clause in Dale's contract with a consulting firm, he was fired from his job as VP. He left town and soon thereafter his ex-wife and children did, too, and they were never heard from again.

What God has put in order, let no man resist.

# SECOND HALF

# non·fic·tion

ˌnänˈfik-shun
*noun*

prose writing that is based on facts, real events, and real people, such as biography or history.

# BICYCLE

I guess I could write a dozen remembrances about my bicycle days. The first would probably be when my brother, Harold, won first prize at a 4th of July contest in Staunton for the Best Decorated Bike. The prize was presented on the stage of the old Strand theater and when they announced his winning, our uncle (Bud) rode it down the aisle while Harold came up to accept the blue ribbon. (It was about this time, circa 1950, that this same brother showed me how to tape little pieces of cardboard in the sprockets of both wheels that would make your worn-out old Schwinn sound like it had a motor.) Boy, we were hot stuff!

I taught myself to ride a bike when I was six years old. We had a gravel driveway and I would stand on a cinder block, I found behind the barn, in order to get astride of it. Once balanced, I would take off pumping until I could no longer keep on the top side of it and then...crash! I would hit those gravels with rocks, skin and blood flying in all directions. I'd walk it back to that cinder block and start the process all over, looking like a car wreck victim after about an hour. And then I rode it everywhere. To church. To the Park. To school. Most times I would just ride for the love of riding. The secondary road by our house would be virtually empty after 5 p.m. every day and on Sundays it was like the main street of a ghost town, so I would just ride and explore and investigate all kinds of trails and paths that really led to nowhere except in a little boy's mind.

One of my most memorable rides:

My dog, King, went everywhere with me. He walked me to the bus stop every school morning and waited there for me every evening. He ran along beside me as I raced all over the neighborhood on my daily adventures. He never left my side. But one day when I was going to the ball diamond and knew I would be there for hours, I scolded him and made him stay

93

home. I can still see him sitting, dejectedly, in the driveway watching me take off up the road. I kept looking back and he just kept sitting there looking lost and more lonesome the farther away I got from him.

To get to the ball diamond, I had to pass the Richmond's house. They were nice people and had a pretty daughter a few years older than me who I liked to look at, but they also had a dog. A big monster dog. A boxer who was usually on a chain in the front yard. He would bark and pull on that chain with the threat of eating me alive every time I passed their house. I was almost past their house this particular day when I suddenly realized I had not heard him bark. I looked over my right shoulder to see why I hadn't heard him and got my answer in a quick glance of fear. He was coming at me silently at full speed and I could see that feral look in his eyes. Without warning he had already decided to have me for lunch. I didn't know whether to peddle faster and try to outrun him (futile) or jump off the bike and meet him head on (stupid).

Thank God and the sweetest old dog a boy ever had, I didn't have to do either. Suddenly all I could see and hear was a flash of teeth and a ferocious growl as King had grabbed that giant boxer in the throat and tumbled him about three times in the dirt. The next thing I heard and saw was him whimpering and limping back toward his own front porch. I jumped off my bike and hugged King long and hard with tears streaming down my face. And then we went back down the road together.

I could play ball any day, but this day I decided to stay home and play with my dog.

# SNOW

I don't like *snow*.

I've never liked *snow*. Even as a kid when it would *snow* two feet and school was called off, I didn't like the *snow*. I liked the day home from school but I stayed in by the radio or TV and never ventured outside unless I was made to put on boots and go get the mail. Or maybe shovel the walk. Or feed the rabbits. (That's an odd clause, isn't it?) But you see we raised rabbits. We had dozens of them in cages and they had to be fed and watered twice a day and when it *snowed* and the temp dropped below 32 degrees, the water in their little tin cans would freeze and I'd have to chisel out the ice and pour fresh water in that would just freeze again in a matter of minutes. Did I say I hated *snow*?

I never liked cold-weather sports. I loved to play softball and baseball but football never held a charm for me. Too cold. And if it started to *snow*, they would just keep playing and my toes and fingers would keep getting colder and I would wish I were someplace else...like inside. I went skiing one time. That was all I needed. Too cold and too much *snow*. I spent most of the evening in the lodge drinking coffee and looking at girls. And every time the door would fly open and a blast of frigid air rushed in, I would cringe and move closer to the fire. I'm just not a wintertime guy.

I've been in cars that slipped all over the *snowy* highways and scared me nearly to my last breath. I've lost traction and have fallen on ice – once breaking my arm. I've never built a *snow*man or cared to. I've never made "angels in the *snow*." I don't even like to pee in the *snow*. It's too cold.

Oh, I've been in a few snowball fights but the most I remember about any of that was how wet my gloves got and how miserably my fingers ached. I always had a sled hanging on the wall of one of our outbuildings but I can only remember using it once or twice in my entire childhood. And I guess the one time that I remember was the one good memory of *snow* I've ever had.

I was eleven or twelve years of age and for some reason my dad, who never really got outside and played with us, decided he was going out after supper and help me make a slick trail down through the *snowy* yard so we could go sledding. My uncle was there. Nen was his nickname. A bachelor uncle who lived with us until his death a few months later. Daddy, Mom, Nen, and my sister, Faye, all went sledding that night for some strange unknown reason. When it got dark, I remember Nen getting a light bulb and extension cord and hanging it on the clothesline so we could keep on sliding down that icy path on the sled. What a night that became to me. The memory of those four people who had never really gotten out and played with me before and here they all were and we were all laughing and having the time of our lives. There are some pictures of us all out there in the backyard in a family album at somebody's house. Maybe mine. I'll have to look for it. I need to see it again to refresh my memory; or maybe not. Because if I'm misremembering it, I don't want to know it.

It was the one time I had fun in the *snow*. Even that long walk back up the slope to start all over again was fun. I can hear each one of their voices in my head this very minute. I can see their faces and I can hear what they were saying. I get tears remembering all this because I loved them all so much.

Nen died a few short months later in one of the outbuildings. The one where the sled was hanging on the wall.

# RAIN

I've never had a mountain retreat or a desert hideaway to run to when I needed to drop a few hours of stress. I've never punched a bag or meditated or even kicked a cat, but I have discovered, over the years, what works for me to get my heartrate back to normal after a particularly trying day at the office. I get in my little convertible, and there have been a number of them, (TR3, Miata, BMW), turn the radio up to a decibel of about ten and let the wind hit me in the face as I drive from one country road to another. This usually happens in the evening after dinner when the sun is beginning to set and the day is winding down.

The beauty and purpose is to literally get lost. I take every turn in the road until I have no idea in heaven or hell where I am or how to get back on familiar ground. This is freeing in every sense and I just love finding new country, bridges, farms, small towns and roadside cafes I've never seen before. Sometimes I wind up 60 or 70 miles from home and have to pull out a map to get me back to a recognizable highway that will take me safely to the house. I've stopped and asked directions more times than you might imagine and by the time I'm back on that good stretch of highway, I have forgotten the rigors of the day and feel like a new and refreshed man ready to whip the world in shape with the next sunrise.

On one of these backroad excursions many years ago, I wound up on something akin to a hard-packed dirt lane in the vicinity of Millboro Springs, VA. I was speeding along with some nostalgia music on the radio, deep in thought about nothing particularly important, when I became aware of a black cloud almost directly overhead. Now any convertible freak or bike rider will tell you they never stop at the first sighting of a cloud. There is always that initial urge to outrun it. It's a high and a thrill. So I hit the accelerator a little harder with that very intention and continued on to nowhere at a pretty good clip.

A big splash on the windshield was the first hint that this race was not going to be won by me. Then a second and a third. I turned the wipers on and kept moving because if you don't stop you don't get wet. This is true unless it is just a drenching rain. The raindrops will blow past you if you keep your speed up and there is nothing to fear until you come to a dead stop. And, of course, that is what you have to do in order to put the top up. Joseph Heller called it a Catch-22. You have to put the top up to stay dry but you have to stop in the pouring rain to put the top up. What to do? What to do? Keep driving until I find a service station? Not in Millboro Springs on a dirt road. Nothing but cornfields and woods on both sides. But what is that coming up on the right? A house. A brick rancher with a carport on the side. And no one was home. Well, at least no car was in the carport and that didn't necessarily mean no one was home. But I'm a poker player and I was willing to take that chance.

I turned swiftly and immediately into the driveway and ran full blast under the carport and slammed on the brakes. Ah, hardly a drop of rain ever touched me. Now if I just raised that top up quickly, I could probably be out of there before anyone looked out and saw me or pulled in behind me and blocked me in. Or worse yet, stepped out the backdoor with a shotgun. Yeah, it looked like shotgun country out there and it looked like they would shoot first and drag me under the porch later.

I was getting the last latch clamped down on the ragtop when I looked out of the corner of my eye and saw the front screen door open. A woman of undeterminable age in an apron stepped partially out and just glared at me. She never said a word and she showed no fear. Threatening would be a better word. I smiled, backed out into the road, waved and yelled, "thank you" while she stood staring at me like a cow in a roadside pasture. What I was doing was probably obvious to her even if it was

# HALF & HALF

annoying to her. She apparently was a nice lady because she showed great restraint by not cussing at me or throwing something harmful at the back of my little car. However, for the next 20 miles I was just waiting for a police car to come in behind me and pull me over for trespassing or worse but, thank the Lord, it never happened. It rained hard all the way home and I never got wet.

Thank you Mrs. Millboro Springs. I was a smart aleck stranger and you gave me shelter.

# TELEPHONE

The first car telephone I ever saw was on the TV show "Richard Diamond" in the late 50s. He had what looked like a regular old black house phone hanging from the center of his dashboard and would get calls from the answering service anytime the plot needed to be moved forward. (The operator was named Sam and you only saw her legs which belonged to a still unknown Mary Tyler Moore.)

The first *real* car telephone I ever saw in person and full color was in the mid-60s. We were doing a television show in Los Angeles and one of the other guests on the show was Otis Redding. Otis had just gotten a car phone (way in advance from anything we would get nearly two decades later on the east coast). He took me out to his vehicle and showed me his mobile phone and how he could call home on it. Wow! He was as pleased as I was impressed.

And I have to admit I have always been beguiled by the cordless, cellular way of life. I had one of the very early "bag phones" in the 80s that sat on the floorboard near the front seat and stayed plugged into the cigarette lighter. If you went in a store and carried it with you, you had to be prepared for someone mistaking it for a purse. Then I graduated to the little flip phone. They got so small if you had one up to your ear, it was nowhere close to your mouth and if you had it near your mouth…well, you get the idea. It worked but I'm not sure how.

Now it's the iPhone and it's not just a phone that is suddenly too big to put in my pocket. It's a still camera, a movie camera, a roadmap, a computer with email and texting, a weather watcher, a full service encyclopedia and even an alarm clock. And I'm a sucker for all its whistles and charms. The number of simple cordless telephones in my house is enough proof of how reliant I am on modern technology. I'm ashamed to state how many

## HALF & HALF

phones are in my home but there is one in every room and in some rooms, two. There's a phone in the garage; in the yard; in bathrooms; a couple in the basement. And if my daddy were alive, I would have to explain why I needed more than one.

One is what we had when I was growing up. It sat in a darken hallway at the foot of the steps and generously served our family of five. I have such wonderful memories of sitting in that telephone chair with the one big wide arm that tabled the phone itself and talking to my friends and my girlfriends. There was only a lamp near the phone and as I would sit there at nights talking, I would always scare and torture myself by constantly looking up those steps at the dark at the top of the stairs. I couldn't look away. But I also couldn't hang up, so there I was in telephone limbo and loving every minute of it.

But as much as I have loved the magic of the telephone down through the years, I have to admit I have received some of the worse news of my life through its receiver. It was over the phone that rang by my bedside at 2 a.m. one August morning in 1967 that brought me the news my father had died. I learned to dread the 2 o'clock hour every night. To this day, I know that is why I look at the clock every time I wake up in the night. I always want to know that 2 a.m. has passed so I can get some uninterrupted sleep.

As much as I love the telephone, I hate its ring. And any ring after 10 p.m. always sends my heart into palpitations. I still expect bad news even though I have made myself a slave to that magical little device of A.G. Bell's.

# BOOKS

A puppy's breath, perfume on the neck of a woman, a lilac bush in the dead of summer, a bakery in the early morning. I love these smells and aromas but maybe my favorite is the olfaction of old books. (Okay, that sounds a little creepy, doesn't it?) And the older and mustier the better. I sniff the pages and take a deep breath and hold it in. If I can find some that have been on a shelf for a dozen decades, ahh, that's even sweeter. New books? Not much to them yet. No character. No body. No really great memories or scents associated with them. I have joked for years that I can smell a book and tell you if it's going to be any good. I've even come to the conclusion it isn't much of a joke. I just love books.

When I was about 30 years old, I had the pleasure of buying an old Italianate, two-story home that was already 98 years old. It had a dark, dank cellar and an attic with pulldown steps and more rooms than any family of four really needed. So I was pleased to find there was still an extra room available even after we had chosen one for my office and one for a sewing room. I knew without too much ruminating what I would love for that room to be. A library! My own personal library where I could surround myself with all my books and just smell and read to my little heart's content with fumes, facts and fiction of days gone by.

In some now-forgotten magazine, I came across a picture of Woodrow Wilson's home in New Jersey. It was a layout of his lawn and landscape and most importantly of his room-by- room interior. And there it was! His library. Dark wood shelves from floor to ceiling covering all four walls. Not a picture on the wall or even a space for one. Just books. Nothing but books from the hardwood floor to the 14-foot ceiling. I loved it. I wanted it. This would be my room of refuge on winter nights when you

HALF & HALF

could see the snow coming down through the window. I would be sitting in my leather chair, reading, with only a dim lamp and maybe a cigar if I so desired. Or sitting in that same chair on a summer afternoon with the window raised and the curtains blowing gently while I read with a glass of iced tea on the end table in close reach. So with just that one picture I proceeded with my plan.

My sons' maternal grandfather, after whom Langdon was named, was a master builder and loved a challenge and any project that hinted at something out of the ordinary. He 'got it' immediately and in a few short months he had gutted the room, reworked the walls, installed the shelves and I had my very own private Wilson library. I would go in there and just stand and smile. I now had all of my books in one room. Nothing scattered over the house that I had to look for when searching for a particular title. I had a History section. A Movie section. Mystery, Biography, Religion and Music sections. All my favorites together at last. I was able to walk into this sanctuary and say to any visitor who cared, "I've read every book in here." (Actually no visitor really cared but it sure was fun for me.)

I felt like Edward Arnold in an old black and white 40's film whenever I sat in there. I felt like a hundred old English parlor dramas when someone would invariably say after dinner, "Let's repair to the library for cigars and brandy." I felt like Woodrow Wilson researching facts for an upcoming speech. I felt like someone I never was but always wanted to be. I loved that room. I never got attached to cars or boats or hobbies of any sort the way most guys do. I never loved a garden or a lawn or hunting or fishing or even had a zeal for sports. But I loved that room with all the passion that most men save for one special love outside of wife and family.

I lived there and enjoyed it daily for the next dozen or so years. And it was hard to leave. All my books in the place where they belonged in that one room. And even though it has easily

103

been 30 years now, I can still remember where each book was; on what shelf; and still see the bindings and spines by just closing my eyes. I even found a little bust of President Wilson that sat on the top shelf overlooking each and every volume, tome and title.

I still have the majority of the books I loved most but I have no idea where the Wilson bust is. In my memory though, I still go there often and rest and read and let one of those dusty old books slump against my chest as I doze and dream.

# GUITAR

Just seeing the word conjures up a thousand memories and images that send me into the past faster than a speeding bullet. There was always one sitting in the corner of the living room at my grandfather's house. It belonged to Uncle Bud and everyone always said of it, "Bud can tune it but he can't play it." He was the only person I ever knew with that particular musical malady but I did know many pickers in subsequent years with the very opposite constraint.

My brother gave me my first one when I graduated from high school. It was a four-string, tenor guitar; quite a popular instrument in the folk/hootenanny craze of the early 60s. I taught myself to play it and never laid it down for two years except to shower and eat. Apparently, I drove my parents crazy with the relentless practice because there is an old familial story that still lingers at family reunions:

*My brother, Harold, came by the house looking for me one day and asked my dad, "Where's Don?"*

*Never looking up from his paper, Dad said, "Ah, he's here somewhere playin' that damn banjo."*

Somewhere in time I switched to the more common six-string guitar and began writing songs. Not particularly good songs, but they served the purpose of helping me find my way into a field that I found fascinating. And if you're a complete songwriter, you have to have an instrument. I fortunately had two. I also taught myself to play chords on a piano during high school, so one day I would write a song with one of those two instruments and the next with the other instrument. I thought I was pretty hot stuff. But the guitar in general and in particular took on a new and special meaning to me in June of 1969.

I never served in the armed forces of any kind, but I have heard television work and the service is alike in the manner of,

105

"Hurry up and wait." And I found this phrase to be true when we joined the cast of the ABC "The Johnny Cash Show" in the summer of '69. We taped each week at the Ryman Auditorium, home of the Grand Ole Opry, in the heart of downtown Nashville. All week we would rehearse and then tape on Thursday nights to a packed house without air conditioning. There is little glory and glamour behind any camera and when it's hot and sweaty it is even less desirable. So the downtime we had during all-day rehearsals and a slow shooting schedule was an invitation to roam the streets of Music City looking for bookstores, music stores, restaurants and air conditioning, just to kill some time.

Right behind the alley from our dressing rooms, there was a pawn shop that always housed interesting things of all makes and matters. And each week there were new items that kept my interest and kept me going back. One was a guitar. Not a used one, but a new one hanging on the wall. It was smaller than a standard size and it had catgut strings that I preferred over the steel strings. From the moment I took it off the wall and held it in my hands, I knew I was taking it home with me. I was writing more songs all the time and I needed something just this size to carry with me on tour, in and out of hotel rooms and theater dressing rooms. It was perfect. It was a Giannini classical model, made in Brazil. It fit my hands and it became my companion and my lover from that moment on. I carried it with me daily all over the world for the next 33 years.

God only knows how many songs I have written but I have had over 250 of them recorded and easily 225 of those were written on that faithful, old, beaten up Giannini. It's a treasure in my heart. And when I retired, so did it. It sits in my office today in a corner with one string broken and it is resting the same as I am. Sometimes I reach over behind my desk and pick it up but never play it. I just touch it and share a few memories

# HALF & HALF

with it and then set it back in its corner like Uncle Bud's that sat in the corner at Granddaddy's house.

It's done its job and it deserves its rest.

# UNCLE

I grew up with five uncles.

Uncle Everett – only saw him once. He died young.

Uncle Howard – always wore a dress hat turned up all the way around. He lived in Dayton.

Uncle Cy – wore a suit and tie every day. He carried a harmonica in his vest pocket and could play the fire out of it.

Bud – a mechanic, always wore a shirt and tie under his coveralls. He was Mom's only brother.

Nen – lived with us. Harold couldn't say "Glenn" when he was little so his name became Nen to him and me. I was closest to him and loved being with him.

Why is it that you call some aunts and uncles by just their name and not others? I always wondered how that came about in families. None of my kids or nieces or nephews use the aunt and uncle titles today. A new generation I suppose. It doesn't necessarily show a lack of respect, but just a shortcut. I have six nieces and nephews and no one calls me uncle.

From my earliest memory, Bud and Nen lived with us. They were always there in the house and I think I viewed them as co-father figures. About the time I was six years old, Bud got married and moved out. Nen left shortly and got a room in town but in a couple of years he was back with us. And I was glad. There was talk he had a girlfriend at the bakery where he worked and I think I saw her once, but it apparently never panned out. He was a bachelor and that is unheard of today. No one is a bachelor anymore. You're either married or assumed gay. Nen was neither; just old-school single.

Nen did a lot of the work around the house and the yard and he let me help him. He showed me how to do stuff that my dad never took time to show me. He was a quiet and easygoing man in every way. He used to check my homework papers at night

# HALF & HALF

and I was constantly amazed at the things he knew with only a fifth grade education. He could tell me if a math problem was wrong and tell me the right answer but couldn't tell me how to work it. He just had an innate knowledge of it and I often thought how brilliant he could have been if only he'd had the opportunity for a higher education. He was Daddy's older brother and right-hand man and my mentor. I followed him around like a little puppy in training.

The last job he had was janitor at our church and I would spend most all of my summer days there with him, helping to clean and mop and dust. I loved being with him as he treated me more as an equal than as a child. He would have made a wonderful father if only he could have conquered that first step of being a husband. But it was never meant to be.

I came home one winter afternoon from school when I was 12 and in the seventh grade. Daddy was at work and mom was in bed as she worked the nightshift at the DeJarnette hospital. Nen was usually there in the kitchen waiting on me, but on this particular day I couldn't find him. I was extremely tired for some odd reason and decided instead of going back out in the cold and looking for him down at the barn or the sheds, I would go lie down in my room. When I awoke about two hours later the house was lighted up in every room except my bedroom. People were milling around noisily downstairs and as I stood on the landing in the staircase, I watched it all as if I were watching a movie screen. People I didn't know coming in and out of the front door; saying things I couldn't quite understand. Then suddenly I saw Mom amid all the commotion and she saw me. She came immediately to me and put her arm around me and said, "Something has happened. Nen has died."

My heart and my mind froze and I can't tell you to this moment what took place over the next couple of hours or even days. But in retrospect, I have tried many times to make sense of it all. I think it was God's work that I was tired and didn't go in

109

## Don Reid

search of Nen that afternoon because when Daddy got home from work that evening, he found him in the feeding shed lying in the floor. He had a .22 hole in his forehead from his own hand. There was no note to anyone and no explanation of any kind. The only thing I have ever been able to make sense of, was the date. It was February 14, 1957. He did this on Valentine's Day and I think only he knew the reason and the need for it.

# FIRE

I am happy to say I have not had many experiences with fire. Never seen anything burning except a bonfire. Never been fired from a job. Never fired a gun at anything besides a target. And I try not to get fired up about too many things now that I'm supposed to be an aged and wise citizen, full of sagacity, clear-headedness and common sense. (Excuse me...I dozed off there for a minute.)

I had a scary experience with fire at the very young age of four or five. We had a large potbellied stove in our living room that basically heated the whole house. Aunts would stand in front of it and hike their dresses in the back to enhance the extreme heat it put off. Dogs would lie behind it and sleep for long winter hours. I remember Daddy and my uncle carrying in buckets of coal to dump into the large mouth of the old iron heater and then stoke it gently until it was red hot and flaming. Mom would sit close to it in a rocker and drink coffee in the mornings. It was a part of the family just as surely as I was. But it became a devil to me.

I'm not sure what I was doing. I may have been playing with the dog or running after a ball or doing whatever a four or five-year old does with his spare time. The simple truth of the matter was I apparently tripped and fell against the stove. It happened so quickly I didn't even put out a hand to brace myself from it. I fell hard against it with the left side of my face. When Mom picked me up, they say you could see my skin stuck to the old potbellied beast. Quick thinking as she was, she grabbed me and took me to the kitchen and rubbed a stick of butter all over my scorched face. I barely cried.

Here are the two mysterious and maybe supernatural elements to that story. I have no memory of this instance whatsoever. It has been told to me by all members of my

111

## Don Reid

immediate family for years. They say it was a horrible moment and everyone worried that I would be scarred for life with a disfigured face. But with my mother's homemade remedy and God's plan, I not only don't remember it, I have no scars or markings. God knew that I would need my face in my work and for some reason known only to Him, He decided to make the butter work.

I know of no doctor who would believe this story and no preacher who wouldn't. But if I can trust my family, it's true.

# FORTUNE

New York City has always been very special to my boys and me. We have been vacationing there since they were pre-teens. We always caught a couple of Broadway shows, cultivated favorite restaurants and would roam the video stores and bookstores into the a.m. I was able to get Langdon on the floor of the New York Stock Exchange when he was only 12, which is a very serious no-no. We discovered Elaine's as a regular after-the-play nightspot for a late meal and always were charmed and entertained by the celebrity clientele. Once when Langdon was about 11 or 12, and trying to decide what to order, someone leaned in from the neighboring table and whispered to him, "Try the lamb chops. They're always good." Turned out to be Darren McGavin. As the years drew on and we would take them with their girlfriends or wives, we would always hit a homerun at Elaine's. Sometimes it would be Michelle Lee or Kirk Douglas and there was always a good story to tell when we got home.

We were planning a trip for the spring of '98 but it wasn't coming together as some of the ladies in the family were unable to go. Debbie suggested it become just a boys' trip and the three of us should go on without them. Her only stipulation was, "you'd better not come back here and tell me you ran into Al Pacino."

So off we took for three days and nights of the Big Apple, just the three of us. And what a ball we had. We ate and talked and smoked cigars in every street side café there was. We caught a couple of really bad plays and each of us even bought a pipe. We laughed and stayed out late and got up early and dug around in the basement of old used record stores and walked the streets until we just couldn't walk anymore. And then one afternoon, on a side street behind our hotel, a sign caught our collective eye at the same time. CLAIRVOYANT – Have Your Fortune Told.

And why not?

I was 53 years old and had never had my fortune told. D. was 30 and had had his told a number of times. Langdon was 23 and game for anything. So in we went to her small apartment, one at a time. Her name was Rose Mark. $20 a pop. She never touched me in any way. She just held her palms a few inches above mine and told me to close my eyes and concentrate on something very dear to me. (This is when I figured I would feel my billfold being slipped out of my back pocket.) After a short time, she sat back and began telling me things about myself. My nature; my family; my marriage. Some things were on the nose, some a little off center but none of it was very far from the truth. It was all very fascinating. At the end of the session she said, "You may ask me any question you would like." Before I could even think of what I wanted to pose to her, I found myself asking, "Are you a Christian?" She said, "Yes, a Catholic." I found some kind of comfort in that.

As I was about to leave, as an afterthought, she gave me a man's name and told me I should avoid him at any cost in any business dealings. (I knew a man by this name and came home and had Butch Hupp, my CPA and business manager, dissolve me of any future dealings with him – just in case.) We all wrote down notes that evening while things were fresh in our minds. Langdon seemed very displeased and skeptical of his reading and D. was his usual tight-lipped, all- smiles self. It was fun and harmless and a wonderful memory.

That night we ate a late supper again at Elaine's and watched a flow of celebrities come and go at tables around us like you wouldn't believe. Robert Altman was holding court to our left. Dennis Hopper was hopping tables all over the place. Alec Baldwin moved from table to table trying to find the one

# HALF & HALF

that gave him the best visibility. And oh, yeah, Al Pacino was at the table on our right.

Maybe I should have just let Debbie tell my fortune and saved $20.00.

# GHOST

Earlier in my life, I was a ghost chaser.

I know my religion warns us to leave it alone as it is possibly of the devil, and I have for the last 30 years. But once upon a time, I got into a clique of like-minded folks and was invited on many ghost adventures. *There are eight million stories in Ghost City; this will be just one of them.*

The call came from a good friend. There was a ghost in a house in Churchville and the family wanted to be rid of it. So this friend and I and my partner, Lew (DeWitt), went out there one night to just sit and talk with the couple who owned and lived in the house. They were full of stories centered around their five-year old's room. They would walk into the room and find all the toys strewn over the floor and then walk back in an hour later and all the toys would be stacked neatly in a corner. Their son, all this time, would have been downstairs playing in the den. The little boy had also told them a number of times about a stranger who occasionally came into his room.

They told us about the loud, single clicking noise that came every night from somewhere in the dining room. Then the creaking on the wooden stairs as if someone were walking up the steps. This happened each night at 10:15 p.m. When daylight savings time sprang forward that spring, it happened at 11:15 each evening. (The ghost had no watch!)

The couple living there informed us the 'entity' liked music. Whenever music was played in the house, it got active and all kinds of knocking sounds could be heard. Well, time for old Don and Lew to swing into action. We went to the car, got a guitar and while I hung out in the dining room at 11:15 waiting for the loud, single click, Lew sat in the stairway and sang a song, the title of which is lost to the ages. What I heard on close observation in the dining room at precisely 15 minutes

# HALF & HALF

after eleven, was the noise of a swinging door directly over the threshold that may have housed a kitchen-to-dining room door of that type in years past. The creaking floor sounds went through the hallway and up the steps toward Lew who was softly singing in wide-eyed anticipation.

At this point, let me remind you of men's fashions of the 1970s. Apache scarfs, bell-bottomed pants, and necklaces. Lew was wearing a choker with little colorful beads. (I probably had something similar around my neck, also.) Just as the creaking reached the step where he was sitting and singing, the choker necklace broke and beads fell and scattered all over the wooden staircase. There wasn't a dry pair of pants in the house.

We went back to their home many times and recorded sounds and made notes and after much research – talking to neighbors, digging into old newspapers, visiting cemeteries – I came up with what we thought was the obvious answer. Twenty years before, a 12-year old boy who lived in the house had died tragically in a tractor accident. The couple felt this was on the nose as they were sure in their minds that the ghost was a young, fun-loving boy. But now, our friend who had originally brought us into this adventure, felt it was time to exorcise the spirit and release him to go on to the "next plane" "toward the light." (His words, not mine. I am strictly a heaven and hell kind of guy.)

We called in a medium we knew who was an ex-Presbyterian minister. A gentle and studious man who sat in a circle with us and some of his cohorts. The lights were low (not to promote spookiness but to keep everyone focused) and we all held hands while he proceeded to go into a trance. He contacted his *guide*, an old Middle Eastern sage, and began talking with a heavy accent. The old sage invited the spirit into our midst and as we were waiting for something to happen, one of the ladies in our circle let out a chilling scream. (She told us later she felt something ice cold go through her and was duly sure it was the ghost.)

117

Don Reid

The sage interviewed the spirit and interpreted his conversation to us as it was happening. And the theory of the 12-year old boy went out the window as quickly as the fat lady's scream had cut through my eardrums. The 'ghost' was an old man who had died fifty years before and had never lived in this house. But he had lived in an old farmhouse that sat on the same site. He was confused and agitated at the young family who had invaded his space. His antics and purpose were to scare them away.

The Presbyterian minister/medium/sage explained death to him, released him and sent him on his way. After he came out of his trance, we, too were sent on our way with a promise of staying in touch. We went a year and never heard from the young family until one day I got a letter from the wife. She told me they were never comfortable in the house after all the events and decided to sell it. She packed all their things herself and they moved to Kentucky. As she was unpacking all their belongings in their new home, she opened one of the suitcases that contained her little boy's clothes and found lying on top of his shirts, in plain sight, a Statler Brothers guitar pick. She assured me firmly she had never seen it before and did not pack it. She asked me, in all sincerity, if this meant the spirit had followed them to the Bluegrass state.

I have to admit I was a little chilled by the turn of events, but assured her I had no idea on God's green earth what that answer would be. I was just a country music ghost chaser and didn't have a clue why a poltergeist would ever want or need a guitar pick. But I'll bet it was for some out-of-this- world Bluegrass picking that I would just love to hear.

# HOMESICK

I never knew what homesick was as a child. I would spend the night at a friend's house and enjoy the experience. I never knew what it was traveling the globe for my work. I often wished I were home for the things I was missing, but I never felt what folks had described to me as homesickness. I guess having my brother and my friends with me on all those trips filled the void. It wasn't until I had retired and was nearly 60 years old that I felt that word hit me with all its force. And it ain't pretty.

I had accepted a speaking and teaching engagement in Troy, Alabama at Troy University. I was to speak there on the topic of songwriting and then stay over for a couple of days and teach and counsel a course on the same subject. Sounded like a good idea and one that I felt capable of handling. One or both of my sons always accompany me on speaking engagements and I looked forward to the trip for a couple of months. Debo was not going to be able to go with us, but Langdon and I were nearly packed and gassing up the car. And then the call came just two days before our scheduled departure and Wilson/Fairchild was booked on a date to fill in for someone who had been touched by a tragedy and Langdon had to fall out. Debbie had church commitments and couldn't be gone for that length of time, so I prepared for the 12-hour journey on my own. I had satellite radio in the car and a stack of CDs; I was loaded for bear.

I wasn't 20 miles out of the city limits when it first hit me. It was like a wave of sickness that grabbed me in the stomach. I felt desperation and a deep sadness like I had never experienced. I shook it off and played the radio. And then ten minutes later it would come over me again. A most lonesome feeling of being away from everyone I loved. A sense of being lost and knowing I'd never be found. A foreboding in my chest and my mind that nothing would ever be the same again. I could even think of my

## Don Reid

dog and get tears in my eyes. I thought maybe I was having an anxiety attack but I really wasn't sure what that was so in time I came to terms with it and realized it was just old fashion homesickness. It hit me in constant waves for the next four days until I was finally heading north to Virginia. I felt like a child and was a little ashamed of myself.

I prayed a lot and listened to a lot of old radio shows until I got home again. It was a pretty miserable trip but I learned the true need and love of family. I've always enjoyed a certain amount of time of being alone, but for some reason unknown to me, this was not meant to be.

I've never felt it since and hope I never will.

# SNAKE

I have never told this story to anyone, especially Debbie. I don't want her to live in constant fear of the worse nor have my friends afraid to come into my house. But here is the gospel truth as it happened.

About three years ago, I was in the kitchen doing the late-night-snack thing that I am cursed with more often than I like to admit. The TV is on, a diet Coke is in my hand and there are cheese and crackers on the counter. I am having a one-man-midnight picnic. Debbie and Lucy, our dog, have gone to bed and the house, except for the kitchen, is dark and quiet. I finish eating, put all my fixings away, turn off the lights and head up the back steps. The moonlight through the windows give off just enough glow that I can see the outline of things but no detail as I make my way toward the top of the stairs. Four steps from the top, I stop and try to focus on something lying in my path. A toy of Lucy's? One that might squeak if I step on it and have her jump off the bed and come running? Or maybe she has had a rare accident that I don't want to step in. So I turn and go to the bottom of the steps and turn on the light.

As I go back up to investigate the item that has interrupted my journey, I see a two-foot black snake stretched out on the step. It isn't moving and neither am I. We both just hold our own without flexing a muscle. As I regain my breath and my heart hits a tempo I can live with, I back down the stairs very slowly. I roll off about three paper towels with one hand and grab a butcher knife with the other. This was all instinct without any real plan of action. Tiptoeing back up the steps, I see that my late-night visitor is still in the same position waiting for me. I creep up quietly and with one quick move I grasp the back of his head with the paper towels. His tail squirms for some sort of purchase but I hold on tight and move quickly back down

121

# Don Reid

the stairs and toward the sink. Holding him with the towels, I put the knife to work and in about two sharp slices, I separate his head from his twitching body. The remains go in the trashcan in the garage and I go to bed with no one else the wiser.

The next day I call the exterminator. I confide in him that I have told Debbie I think I saw a mouse and I want him to stick to that story while he investigates the entire house and secures it from any other critters making an entrance. He goes along with my devious plan and all is well and pretty much forgotten about by me in a few days.

Two weeks later, Debbie walks into my office from her bathroom and says, "Is this some sort of joke or is it real?" What? I follow her to her bathtub and there lounging like a bathing beauty is a three-foot black snake, probably kin to the one I executed a few short weeks ago. I go for the same knife and paper towels and repeat my modus operandi and act as shocked as she does. I still didn't want to tell her about the first one because I didn't want her to think it would ever happen again. And it hasn't. Thank God and the Nagy Exterminating Company. I called him back and he double sealed the house and now we live a relative quiet and uneventful life style. But I never walk up those back steps by moonlight glow anymore. I use every light switch in the house as I go from room to room.

# SUMMER

Growing up, our family never went on a vacation in the summer the way most families did. The months of June, July and August really spelled freedom more than vacation and between you and me, I loved it. Stayed up late at nights, slept in late in the mornings and then just roamed and did as I pleased. I was home a lot by myself as my mother pulled a night shift and slept during the day and my dad was at work. My brother and sister were older and working, so it was just me and King, my dog, and my bike. And friends that were willing to roam with me.

Every June there was Bible School from nine to twelve just up the road at our church. I rode my bike and then stayed afterward and played ball all afternoon at the diamond just behind the Sunday school building. There was also a small grocery store just beside the church, so there were enough popsicles and soft drinks consumed in a day's time to kill an army of normal kids. But we survived.

It was about 2 p.m. and my friend, Doug, and I were just leaving that grocery store on our bikes, heading home. I had a Grapette drink in my right hand and a handlebar in my left and as we pulled out toward the road, my bike skidded on the gravel shoulder, toppled over and threw me off. I went flying, unfortunately, into the westbound lane of Route 250 with a large Pepsi Cola truck bearing down on me. He slammed on his breaks and missed me by inches as I lay in the center of the road, still gripping my Grapette. As you might imagine, this drew quite a crowd and caused quite a commotion. Traffic stopped, people ran from the little two-employee grocery store, and the truck driver and other drivers came to my aid. But I was okay. I was sound and a little scared but I got up and rode my bike home and needless to say, finished my Grapette.

When I got home, I was a little more shaken than I thought I was so I went to my room and stretched out on my bed and went to sleep. Less than an hour later, I opened my eyes to my my mother sitting on the edge of my bed, gently shaking me awake. Someone had called her and told her what happened and she had gotten up to see to me. All I remember her saying was, "You should never go to sleep if there is any chance you bumped your head. Do you feel okay?" I assured her I did and she made me get up and move around instead of going back to sleep.

It was 55 years before I realized why all this happened. This single instance gave me the pivoting moment I needed to plot my 2010 novel, *One Lane Bridge*. On pages 288 and 289 you can read my fictionalized version of that "wreck on the highway." But, oh, what a summer! Ballgames, soft drinks, bike wrecks and a mother's love and comfort. I'd give $50 for a Grapette right this minute.

# SPAGHETTI

I love Italian food but I can't tolerate garlic. So you can easily see my dilemma. It is a near impossible feat to sit down at an Olive Garden and ask them to hold the garlic. It's a little like going to a hockey game and asking not to see blood. It just ain't gonna happen. So my favorite way of eating ravioli, lasagna, manicotti, rigatoni or spaghetti is to eat it at home where I know my wife will leave out or add in whatever I request. To say the least, I am not a purist when it comes to ethnic food. I guess you could best describe my leanings as American/Italian dishes. I love the other spices. I love the sauces. I love how I feel when I finish a plate of my favorite pasta. (I actually crave a cigar and two Zantacs within minutes of any Italian meal. But I gave up the cigars years ago, darn it.)

Debbie and I were switching channels one night years ago, looking for a movie to watch when we came across one just starting that grabbed our interest. It was obviously an independent and near art film starring Stanley Tucci who also wrote and directed it. (Of course it was an independent if it starred Stanley Tucci. His name will sorrowfully never be as big as his talent.) Tucci and his brother, played by Tony Shalhoub, another actor whom the public has never recognized properly, had opened a restaurant on the New Jersey Shore in the late 1950s. To get the name of their newly founded business in the paper and get some free news space, they thought they had it all set and arranged to have entertainer Louis Prima and his entourage come in for dinner on this particular *Big Night*. (This was the title of the 1996 movie and the entire script was built around this dream possibility.) But in the ensuing days and hours of preparation for the singer's arrival, we saw many meals served and many customers come and go. And here was the absolute hook for Debbie and me.

We had never seen so much food look so good. Every meal was shot to its best positioning. People eating and drinking and eating some more and we just looked at each other and laughed at how much we wanted to join in and eat with them. I finally said to her, "Do we have any spaghetti in the house?" Eleven o'clock, one hour before midnight, and I was ready to cook up a pot before bed. It had the same effect on me that the scene in *The Godfather* always has on me. Clemenza is making spaghetti sauce in the kitchen and all those guys are sitting around the table with bread in hand, sucking up spaghetti. I can hardly stand it. I wanted spaghetti and I wanted it now. But we had to wait until the next evening at suppertime. But Debbie fixed it and lots of it, just the way I like it.

We still laugh about the movie and the yearning we both had watching it. Pretty good little film and you'll have to check it out to see if Louis Prima, indeed, ever shows up.

# ACCIDENT

I was the guest speaker in a Presbyterian church recently and told this story at the morning service. The point of it being that God is in everything that happens to us and is the overseer of all outcomes. (That's how we Presbyterians roll.)

I was 15 years old. I knew less than nothing about anything, but I had a driver's permit and that made me equal. (Yes, we could have a driver's license at 15 years of age at that time. Dangerous times, it was.) It was a hot summer day and I was riding through the streets of Staunton going wherever the day would take me. As I passed a particular house in a residential area, two girls were on the front porch in shorts and they waved at me. Hey, I'm 15 years old. I waved back. And just kept on waving as I continued driving past their house. When I looked back around to see where I was headed, I was headed straight at the car coming toward me. I swerved quickly but still side swiped the oncoming vehicle, tearing off the side mirror and that whole chrome strip that ran down the side of the front door.

The driver of the other car was the nicest old gentleman you would ever want to meet. I remember his name was Mr. Jones and he was very understanding, (more so than my daddy was) and we exchanged insurance cards and phone numbers. The police were called and an officer came and wrote up the ticket, handed it to me and told me to be in traffic court in ten days.

Ten days later, I walked into the courtroom scared to death. I had never been in court in my life. The closest I had ever been was watching Perry Mason on TV. When my name and case were called, I walked up to the front and looked up at the judge who was looking down on me from his majestic pedestal in his flowing black robe. He said, "Alright, son, tell me in your own

# Don Reid

words what happened with this accident you had. What were you doing and what was Mr. Jones doing?"

With all of the honesty and courage I could muster up, I swallowed hard and said, "Well, your honor, I was driving in the middle of the road and Mr. Jones was trying to get away from me."

At this point, I suddenly heard a voice behind me say, "Just a minute, Judge." I looked around and it was the police officer who had been there that day on the scene and had written up the summons. My heart sank as I was sure what he had to say to the judge was not going to be helpful to me any way. But he continued by saying, "That is a very narrow street over there, Your Honor, and they have cars parked on both sides of the street and then traffic going both ways. It's a real tight squeeze and it's no wonder this young man had a problem getting through there. It's a situation we need to look at and correct in that block."

My heart came back with a flutter and stuck in my throat. What had I just heard? This policeman had just come to my defense when I thought he was coming to bury me. My eyes were going from the officer to the judge when I heard the judge say, "Alright, boy, that'll be ten dollars. Pay up out front and get out of here." And I did just that as fast as I could.

I have thought about this accident and this court incident many times through the years and, with age, I realized how differently it could have gone. You see I had a job at the time bagging groceries at a local grocery store, so I had ten dollars, and all was well. But so easily Mr. Jones could have been angry in that courtroom and been up in my face shaking his fist. The police officer could have said to the judge, "This kid has no business being behind the wheel. Waving at girls instead of watching where he was going." And the judge could have said, "Alright boy, that will be $100. Pay up out front and get out of here."

128

## HALF & HALF

Well, as I said, I had the $10 but I wouldn't have had the $100. I had never seen $100. And I could have left that court in debt with a sour taste for the judge and the law in general. So quickly my whole life could have been different.

But this accident had a long-term effect on me. As I related to you earlier, I told this very story recently at a Sunday morning church service because sitting in the choir at that service was the 84-year-old retired policeman who came to my defense that day in court. His name is Harvey Hickman and we became friends through the years.

Thank you, Harvey. And God is truly the overseer of all outcomes.

# PANIC

Christmas is a big deal in our family and at our house. Debbie starts decorating Thanksgiving night. She, Debo and Langdon put up three trees. (I'm pretty useless, as you already know, and a terrible decorator.) We go on family shopping trips; we have an open house about a week before Christmas Day for all our extended family and special friends; we attend services and programs at both our churches and we never stop and take a breath until Christmas night. We love every minute of it.

We have lots of traditions we try to maintain and re-enjoy every year. One of our favorites starts early morning on Christmas Eve. With the kids (D. and Julie and Langdon and Alexis) and the four grandchildren (Caroline, Sela, Davis and Adra), we all go out to breakfast at the Stonewall Jackson Hotel and then come back to Grammie and Poppy's (that would be Debbie and me) and have Christmas at our house. The grandkids have told us this is their favorite part of all the holiday season. They love the hotel and the early morning gathering because the lobby is adorned with a large tree and big, bright ornaments and lots of color. Just a festive and fun place to be on Christmas Eve.

So, on one of those special mornings, a few years ago, we finished breakfast in the hotel dining room and some of the grandkids wanted to explore the hotel. They always like me to take them up on the mezzanine so they can look over the railings at the lobby from an overview angle. Davis was five years old then and as we were walking around and looking at the beautiful sights and they were telling me what they liked most about the season, I suddenly noticed he was missing.

"Where's Davis?" I asked his sister and his cousins. And yes, being the worrywart I naturally am, there was already a little panic in my voice.

130

## HALF & HALF

One of them answered (I don't remember which one) and said, "I think he just got on the elevator."

"What?" This was definitely me and panic was growing.

I ran to the elevator, saw the door closing, and got just a glimpse of him standing calmly looking up at all the glowing buttons. I started pushing the Open Door button and pushed about a thousand times in ten seconds. Just for your information, pushing one of those buttons repeatedly and frantically will not make the door open any quicker. It won't even make it open at all. My mind was racing. A five year old boy is in a hotel elevator going to heaven knows what floor all by himself. He probably can't reach the buttons and I was already letting my imagination rage with all the dangers he could be in.

"You girls go get your dads. Tell them to come right now."

As they ran off down the steps to do as I told them, I tried to decide if I should stay on this floor in case he came back down or run the steps to each floor to see if I could find him. I was getting hot inside my clothes with indecision and just as I was wiping December perspiration from my forehead, the elevator door opened. I ran to it just in time to see a man and woman exit it.

"Have you seen a little blonde haired, five-year old boy?" I asked hurriedly.

"Yes," they assured me. "He got off on the fifth floor."

At this point, I hear Debo and Langdon coming up the stairs behind me. I started barking out orders.

"One of you stay here in front of the elevator. The other one, run up the steps and check all the odd numbered floors. I'll go to all the even numbered floors. We can't miss him that way." I was so afraid he might be scared and lost or worse yet, in some sort of unmentionable danger and I knew it was all my fault for letting him get away.

Both my sons are much less excitable than I am and they both assured all the family, who was now gathering on the

131

## Don Reid

mezzanine, that everything would be okay and that no one should panic (especially me).

Then, as if by answered prayer, the doors of the Stonewall Jackson Hotel elevator flew open and there stood, all smiles and Christmas cheer, my little blonde haired grandson. I grabbed him and hugged him much to his bewilderment; the family all had a laugh on me; and my panic subsided, leaving me only with a wet shirt, a fluttering heart and a pretty darn good feeling clear down to my toes.

He had gotten off on the fifth floor, as we had been told, walked around and looked around and then reached the button and gotten back on and had come calmly down to the lobby. He was having fun, was in a great mood, and was puzzled by all the commotion and concern.

I do remember one last thing. I reached down, swooped him up in my arms, and said, "Let's go home. This boy needs some Christmas presents."

# TEACHER

Junior Year in High School – Charles Duff

He taught the only Creative Writing class Wilson Memorial High ever had. He was young and different and loyal to his own style. He was a rebel and we all took refuge in him. He wore a tie each day in a manner that showed defiance while still conforming to the dress code. His eyes were wild with excitement and they would dart about as if he were looking for an opening in the real world that he could jump through. He loped around the room with great flair as he lectured and gave us tips on what to write and how to write it. He gave us such creative and interesting assignments. He told us once, "Write me some pages tonight on anything you want. But I don't want you to write about the rainy streets of Paris because none of you have been there. *Write What You Know!*" Those four words have been engraved in my mind all of my writing career. No better advice can be given to any writer. I even made a little sign years later and hung it on one of my desk drawers where only I could see it. It simply said to me *Write What You Know!* I saw it every day and it sank in. I used that advice in every creative situation I ever faced, whether it was writing songs, a TV script, a comedy routine, a book – fiction or non-fiction.

He drilled in us that content was more important than length. If you can say it in a page and make it powerful and meaningful and interesting, that's great! Don't stretch it out to three pages just to fill up space. Know when you've said it all. A favorite assignment I remember so well was, "Look out that window. You see a brick wall out there. Describe to me in detail that brick wall as if you were describing it to someone who has never seen a brick wall." He made us think about things we never thought about and I left that class completely in awe of the guy. But all stories don't have a happy ending.

(Did you notice what I did there? I ended a paragraph with a sentence that made you want to read the next paragraph. That's the kind of stuff he taught me.)

Now to understand this story completely, you have to understand the music business I was in for forty years. Hardly a night went by, when we were on tour, that someone didn't come to the stage door and try to get in to see one of us with a bogus story of being an old friend. Some would even tell our manager, "We know them well. We're all from Staunton," (pronouncing it the way it's spelled instead of plain old Stanton.) That was always a dead giveaway. Or they would say they went to school with all of us, which was impossible considering our age differences. So it was really a rarity for a legitimate friend to show up and leave a believable message. But one night one did.

Just before we were about to walk on stage, our manager said to me, "Don, a Charles Duff was at the backdoor. Said he was a teacher of yours many years ago. I told him to come back after the show and you'd meet with him." Yes he was and yes I will. I had lost track of him for the past twenty plus years and I was thrilled he was here. I couldn't think about what I was doing on the stage for thinking about him and how excited I would be to talk to him again, this time as an adult. All through the show I kept searching the audience for his face but never found him. But when the final song ended, I rushed back to the stage door, flung it open, looked both ways, waited, looked again…and he never showed up.

End of story. He never showed up. What a disappointment. I wanted so badly to tell him how much he had meant to me and my writing career. I have over 250 songs recorded by many different artists and I used techniques in every one of them taught to me by him. I've had seven books published and I used exercises and applications on every page he had instilled in me. I have no idea where he is today, but I would love to tell him how much he meant to me and my life. He was a good and generous teacher.

Thanks, Charlie Duff, wherever you are.

# RING

Downtown Staunton, Virginia was a different place when I was 14 years old than it is today. Where there were local shoe stores, newsstands, dress shops and haberdasheries, today you see only gift shops appealing to the tourist; coffee houses appealing to the leisured; and craft stores appealing to mostly no one. Where there used to be busy sidewalks and bag-carrying shoppers, today there are a few folks walking the streets with little in their hands. I still love it. It's still my hometown, but it has changed, as has every small town in our ever-changing country.

When I was 14, I would come to town for everything I needed. School clothes, school supplies, sneakers, a new sport coat, sports equipment, and records. There were even two large grocery stores downtown, one on the main street, and numerous small Mom and Pop grocery stores on nearly every corner. The reason for my trip that afternoon after school is now long forgotten but I do remember wandering into the jewelry store on the corner of Beverley and New Streets.

The manager there talked to me and let me linger over the watches and the ID bracelets and cuff links and rings. I liked everything I saw but I was drawn to one particular ring. The manager, who I later came to know as Carl Durham, told me that ring was called a Cat's Eye. He took it out of the glass case and let me put it on my finger. I stretched my arm out, clenched and unclenched my fist and knew that this Cat's Eye ring looked pretty darn good on my hand. Of course, the first question I asked was the price. Wish I could remember exactly the dollar amount but what I do remember was it was well out of my range. I had a job after school on Fridays and all day on Saturdays bagging groceries at the Farm Bureau Co-op, so I was pulling down about $15 dollars a week. However, that wasn't

136

# HALF & HALF

near enough to afford this ring that was looking better to me by the second. So I handed it back and thanked Mr. Durham and headed on down the street.

Every few days, whenever I was in town, I would stop in the jewelry store and admire it and usually Mr. Durham would pull it out of the case and let me wear it around the store. After about three or four trips like this, he asked me just how much I was making a week. I told him and he looked at me awhile and said he thought we could work something out. That day before I left the store, he gave me the ring and had me sign a sheet of paper saying I would come by and give him $2.00 every week until the Cat's Eye was paid for. What a great deal for me and what a horrible deal for him.

I was too young to know it at the time, but I later learned that a 14-year-old could not enter into a legal contract. Of course, Mr. Durham knew that and was simply taking a chance of faith on me. I wore the ring home and without fail I went by every Monday and gave him $2.00 until that two-toned, yellow and gray jewel was mine, all mine.

I looked back on that event many years later and marveled at what he did for me. The piece of paper meant nothing. Had I never come back and paid the second $2.00 payment, there was nothing they could have done to me. I had a credit reference way before I was even a legal credit risk. He trusted me and gave me a break that few kids my age ever get. And why? Because he was a good man and he had a good heart.

Carl Durham opened his own jewelry store a few short years later just across Beverley Street and it still stands there today. Carl is gone now, but the store is called Crown Jewelers just as he named it and I have seldom bought a piece of bling from anyone else in my life. He did for a kid what I hope I have taken the time to do somewhere along the way. He taught a lesson by wearing his heart on his sleeve so I could wear that ring on my finger. He was a good man and Staunton misses him.

# KEY

New York, Manhattan in particular, has always been a favorite vacation spot for my family. It's close enough from home (6 hours) to drive and a long weekend in the Big Apple is always fun no matter what the weather may be. We like to shop, catch a couple of Broadway plays, eat at new restaurants, but always at a couple of our old favorites, and then just walk the streets and enjoy the sights. We even have a favorite hotel, the Park Lane, where we have stayed for years. All the staff calls all the family by their first names and we call all of them by theirs. Sort of a homey touch for the big city.

One of the offerings of the house is the rental of a small, personal deposit box behind the desk in the lobby. For a nominal fee, you can leave cash or jewelry or whatever you desire in this little safe and then the singular key is given to you for the duration of your stay. They always stress the fact that even the hotel does not have a second key. One key for each safe and that's it. This way you are assured of the security of your items. We always get one box and everyone puts whatever they desire in there for safekeeping.

It could have been anywhere that I lost the only key to box number 12. In one of the eateries we frequented; and there were lots of them. Or maybe it was lodged in one of the seats of one of the theaters after slipping out of my pocket. In a cab. At Macy's. At Saks. Bloomingdale's. The possibilities are staggering. All I know for sure is that when I went to the front desk of the hotel to check out on Sunday afternoon, I discovered I no longer had the key that had been entrusted to me.

"Certainly you have a backup key back there someplace, don't you?"

# HALF & HALF

But the very courteous desk clerk assured me he didn't. He even called the day manager who came out and very sympathetically reinforced the clerk's position.

"Has this never happened to anyone else before?" was my next question.

Oh, yes, I was assured. It has and does happen rather regularly. And there is a common procedure to getting the safe open. The manager explained that all they had to do was call a local locksmith who would come downtown, drill into the door of the safe, cut the lock from the door and then replace it with a new lock. The standard cost for this was usually in the $250 range. "Of course, Mr. Reid, that entire expense is yours as you are the one who lost the key."

And as it should be, I agreed it was my fault and I would pay the price. Just go ahead and make the call so we can check out and get on our way. But as nothing usually is, it wasn't as easy as it sounded. After about an hour of phone calls, the manager came very sheepishly out to where I had been sitting and waiting in the lobby. "Mr. Reid, we are having a great deal of trouble finding a locksmith willing to come downtown on a Sunday afternoon. Most are giving us a flat no, yet a few are giving us exorbitant and inflated prices. If you are not willing to stay till morning and you have to check out this afternoon, it is going to cost you."

"How much?"

"A pretty penny."

I remember him actually saying this. And I remember looking at him directly in the eye and asking, "How pretty?"

I am embarrassed to tell you what it cost me to get out of that hotel that Sunday. I best remember it cost me nearly as much as the cash I had in the safe. I would have been just as well off to have left town and let the hotel keep whatever they found in the deposit box when they got a reasonable locksmith the next day. But it was my doing, so I took the knocks.

Don Reid

Somewhere in NYC, someone found that key on the floor of Sardi's, Sparks Steak House or maybe the Barrymore Theater, picked it up and wondered what it went to. They may have turned it in to management or they may have just absently put it in their pocket. It may be laying in someone's old desk drawer this very day. Someone will pick it up years from now and think, "Wonder what this old key is to?"

Well, buddy, I can tell you what it's to and I can also tell you what it's worth. But I won't. However, I'll tell you the lesson I learned. Just put your extra cash in your shoe and take your chances on the streets of New York.

# CHARITY

Route 250 runs into, through and out the other end of Staunton, VA. I grew up on this road. It ran in front of the house, heavy with traffic day and night. In back of the house, we had a large yard, a vegetable garden and plenty of room for a boy of any size to roam and explore. There was an apple orchard directly behind our property which supplied me with more than enough trees to climb. And then came the train tracks. This was the dramatic railway for the freight and passenger trains that broke through the night and raced through the dawn with a noise that becomes unnoticed after a short while. Folks would always ask, "Don't those trains wake you up at night?" Heavens no, my whole family would reply. You get used to it. After awhile you don't even hear them.

We, my friend Bobby and I, used to hang out on the edge of the orchard and wave at the engineer as he passed by on the midday run. We were six and seven years old and would jump around and laugh with joy if he waved back. Some didn't. Can you imagine such a curmudgeon who wouldn't wave back at a couple of kids so excited to see a locomotive and a big-time engineer? I guess he was busy driving a train or something.

There must have been a slow spot along the tracks close by our house; maybe a big curve was coming up or a hill was about to be ascended, because it seemed to be a jumping off and jumping on spot for the hoboes. These out-of-work travelers were the homeless of today. They were products of the Depression from twenty-some years before. Vagabonds and vagrants and men just simply down on their luck. Some could be trusted, some couldn't. Like all walks of life, preachers, pirates or country music singers, they were a fair mixture of good and evil. You couldn't judge them by their clothes or by the look in their eyes. On any given day, you'd be wrong as often as right.

141

# Don Reid

These hoboes had a code of their own that provided a sense of safety for all of them. They would leave signs along properties for any of their brothers who came along behind them, letting them know the lay of the land. I understand they had a shorthand of their own; markings that warned and informed one another. A marking, maybe in chalk, somewhere near a house of /// would mean a friendly doctor lives here. There were also markings to let each other know that this homeowner had a gun. One that meant this homeowner is not friendly toward us. And there was the one that I am sure was marked somewhere down in that orchard to signify our house though I personally never ran across it. But by the evidence of all of those bindle-carrying drifters who knocked on our backdoor, I'm sure someone had drawn a picture of a cat. It may have been a rough caricature on a rock, but I'm sure it was there. The 'cat' meant a kind woman who will feed you lives here. And she did.

More than once, my brother and I would hear that rap on the screen door and Mom would go to the back porch and find one of these men standing in rags and asking, "Could you spare me a sandwich?" And invariably she would fix him one along with a glass of iced tea and hand it out the door. He would sit in the backyard under a tree and eat while my brother and I sat under another tree and watched him in silent awe. He would finish his sandwich and leave his glass setting in the grass or maybe hand it to one of us. Then he would gather his few belongings and we'd watch him disappear down the back path, through the orchard, waiting on the next train to slow down for the curve ahead. This was the early 50s. A less dangerous time. A time before there was such fear that would keep you, today, from even opening the door.

My mother was a hero among many others who did the same for those in need. And it's a shame today that we can't, for our own safety, do likewise. But who would even think of opening a door to a stranger with a young mother and two or

## HALF & HALF

three kids in the house? The biggest part of this charity was not just her loving nature, but her trusting nature.

A sweet memory of a sweet gesture of a sweet woman from a simpler time.

# ABOUT THE AUTHOR

Don is one of the original members of The Statler Brothers, the most award-winning act in the history of country music. He and his brother and two friends began singing in their hometown of Staunton, Virginia when Don was only fourteen years old. They were discovered in 1964 by Johnny Cash and given their first record contract. By the time Don was twenty years old, the Statlers had their first major, world-wide hit with "Flowers On the Wall" which started a string of hits that generated a career in the music industry that lasted four decades. The Statlers have been the recipients of multiple industry awards:

- 3 Grammy Awards
- 9 CMA Awards
- 48 Music City News / TNN Awards
- 13 Gold Albums
- 8 Platinum Albums
- 1 Double Gold DVD

Don was the principle writer for the group with over 250 songs recorded by the Statlers as well as Johnny Cash, George Burns, Tammy Wynette, The Cathedrals, and Elvis Presley, to name a few. He personally has won 18 BMI awards, which are given to the writer for the most songs played on the radio each year.

For the next thirty-eight years, the Statlers continued to dominate the concert circuit with sold out houses. In the 90s, The Statlers hosted a music variety show, "The Statler Brothers Show" on TNN for seven years. This series was produced by the Statlers with each episode written by Don and his brother, Harold. This show was ranked #1 on cable television for all

144

# HALF & HALF

seven years. The Reid brothers also wrote another TV series called "Yesteryear" as well as numerous television specials.

The Statler Brothers were inducted into the Gospel Music Hall of Fame in 2007. In 2008, they were inducted into the Country Music Hall of Fame. They are one of only six  acts to reside in *both* Halls.

Since the music group's retirement in 2002, Don took to writing books. He has had seven other books published with this one being his eighth. And probably more to come.

Don and his wife, Debbie, live in Staunton with their faithful cocker spaniel, Lucy. He lives close to his two sons and takes his grandchildren to school every morning.

Made in the USA
Las Vegas, NV
01 April 2021